**Jake glanced** [...]
**'You're nervo** [...]

Olivia lifted her he[...] [...]antly at the assured, handso[...] [...]ace. 'I'm...' She had been about to deny it—pointlessly, of course, because they both knew she *was* nervous. 'I...don't know you.' She shrugged awkwardly. 'And yet I find myself drawn into deep conversations that...that disturb me... and...' She closed her mouth abruptly. What on earth had possessed her to be so frank... and to a perfect stranger?

**Laura Martin** lives in a small Gloucestershire village with her husband, two young children and a lively sheepdog! Laura has a great love of interior design and, together with her husband, has recently completed the renovation of their Victorian cottage. Her hobbies include gardening, the theatre, music and reading, and she finds great pleasure and inspiration from walking daily in the beautiful countryside around her home.

**Recent titles by the same author:**

A STRANGER'S LOVE

# PERFECT STRANGERS

BY
LAURA MARTIN

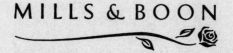

MILLS & BOON

MILLS & BOON and the Rose Device
are trademarks of the publisher.
Harlequin Mills & Boon Limited,
Eton House, 18–24 Paradise Road, Richmond, Surrey TW9 1SR

© Laura Martin 1996

ISBN 0 263 79450 4

Set in 10 on 12 pt Linotron Times
01-9604-54262

Typeset in Great Britain by CentraCet, Cambridge
Made and printed in Great Britain

# CHAPTER ONE

THE journey had tired Olivia more than she had
anticipated. She had been craning her neck over the
last few miles, like a child on a day trip to the sea,
waiting and watching for that first magic glimpse of the
cottage. She smiled to herself. Mad. But then, it was a
good sign. It meant that her dream hadn't palled in the
intervening weeks. It meant, surely, that she was still
doing the right thing.

She forced herself to lean back in the taxi. The
countryside was as wonderful as she had remembered
on her fleeting visit a few weeks ago. Still green and
lush. The daffodils hadn't been properly open then. . .
now they seemed to be everywhere, so bright and
cheerful; yellow bunting welcoming Olivia to her new
home.

The taxi driver was youngish with sandy hair. Something about the back of his head reminded her of Paul.
Olivia's eyes rested unseeing on the tanned neck and
slightly wavy hair, and for a moment her thoughts spun
the one hundred miles or so back to London. This time
last week, she thought, I was sitting at my large glossy
desk, wearing my high-powered suit, playing executives. Being someone else. Pretending. Trying desperately not to think of Paul as a husband—somebody
else's husband. . .

She had broken her first rule—no thinking about
Paul, or London, or the life she had left behind.

Olivia shook herself mentally and focused on the

passing countryside, glancing anxiously up at the patchy sky because there were dark clouds looming on the horizon.

'Do you think it will rain?'

The stocky denim shoulders in front lifted slightly, surprised maybe at being addressed. 'Don't know, love; maybe. Those clouds don't look too promising, do they?'

'Do you live near here?' Oliva asked, determined to strike up a relationship of sorts with someone local. That was one thing she had promised herself. Integration with the community. She would be no commuter, living in the country, working in the city—not that she had a job at all now. She took a deep breath. Eight years of working her way up the ladder, reaching the top rung and then throwing herself off into the abyss of unemployment below.

'No.'

It wasn't much of a start. The taxi driver swung the rather aged car around a bend too quickly and with not a lot of finesse.

Almost there.

She blinked and the village with its pub and school and tiny shop had been passed. Just a few more minutes and she would see the cottage, *her* cottage; thatched and quaint, with little leaded windows and roses around the door—well, maybe not exactly roses, she amended swiftly, more likely weeds, but still looking wonderful, still hers. . .

Olivia leant forward and offered the directions, written down by the estate agent on her first visit at the end of March, to the taxi driver. 'Perhaps it's best if you look at them,' she murmured. 'I never was very good at navigation and there are so many different turnings around here.'

They were travelling along a winding lane with high hedges on either side now. The car was flung around another bend, and then the taxi driver glanced down, just for a second, and in that moment, seemingly out of nowhere, there appeared a large, immaculate black Range Rover.

It all happened so quickly. Olivia, already perched on the edge of her seat with her crumpled directions, was jolted forward as brakes squealed, the car swerved and a slow-motion impact took place. She winced as the side of her face came into contact with the vinyl-covered seat in front and spent a moment or two in dazed disbelief, aware of a stream of curses spewing forth from the taxi driver's lips.

Olivia released a shaky breath, rubbing gingerly at her sore cheek, and watched miserably as the taxi driver wrenched open his door and marched aggressively over to the other, far more opulent vehicle.

The door of the Range Rover was opening. Tinted windows gave it a somewhat mysterious air as well as keeping out prying eyes, and it was a few moments before the other driver emerged.

What had she expected? A local farmer with ruddy cheeks and a cloth cap? Or maybe an irate woman with a tight perm and strings of pearls swinging angrily over an ample bosom?

Olivia found herself drawing a deep breath. Not this. Definitely not someone like this.

Unexpected exhilaration coursed through her body, as six feet plus of successful, handsome male personified came into full view.

Ignoring the taxi driver, who hovered menacingly,

the man bent and without haste examined the damage to his vehicle.

Glossy black hair, ruffled by the chilly breeze, fell over one eye and a large tanned hand smoothed it back from his strong, tenacious face.

Olivia felt a prickle of excitement run through her. She knew she was staring, but somehow she didn't seem able to help herself. Her eyes wandered over the rust suede jacket, the cream open-necked shirt, resting for a fraction of a second longer on the chocolate-brown corduroy trousers that fitted well enough to define the powerful shape of well-muscled thighs.

If this had been London instead of the Oxfordshire countryside, if she had still been editor of the best glossy magazine in town, she would have got out of the car and offered him a modelling assignment on the spot, *any* assignment—it wouldn't have mattered what.

Olivia's lips twitched slightly; not that he would be the type to accept such a proposition—she recognised strength of character when she saw it—but it would have been well worth the try, if only for the chance of making contact with such a man.

Cautiously she opened the door of the taxi and got out.

'You were travelling too fast.'

His voice didn't mar her first impression of authority and power and success. Deep, with a gravelly masculine undertone that brooked no argument. Precise, too. Direct.

Olivia glanced briefly across to witness the reaction of the bullish, red-faced taxi man and then her eyes were fixed once more on the magnificent face.

'Now just you look here!' The taxi driver's tone and demeanour were depressingly predictable. Olivia stood silently, unable to drag her gaze away from the formidable figure, as the driver's aggressive tone filled the chilly spring afternoon air.

What was wrong with her all of a sudden? she wondered. Had the bump to her face done some *real* damage? Stop staring like a besotted idiot! she chided silently. You've come across a thousand handsome men before! But not like this. Olivia inhaled a breath and tried to steady her breathing. This man was different.

'You were driving too fast and you know it.' The slightly hooded gaze was as direct as the words used, the deep voice clipped and assured. 'This is a narrow country lane, not the M25. Just give me your name and insurance details and quit the bluster. I'm not going to waste my time arguing with you.' He glanced with irritation at the slight dent in the Range Rover's bumper. 'You're lucky; the damage to my vehicle is negligible, so your bill won't be too extensive.'

'I'm *lucky*? Now wait a minute!' The flabby face turned a deeper shade of puce. The taxi driver moved forward angrily, and for a moment Olivia thought he was going to lose his temper completely and actually embark on physical violence. A disastrous course of action. Surely he could see that? she thought. One blow from that tall, powerful physique and the pugnacious little man would be laid out cold.

'You have a passenger, I see.' The dark, arrogant gaze was flicked in Olivia's direction. She burned as he studied her face, feeling the flames of awareness rising as if he had touched her, as if. . .as if he had done more than that. Such eyes, she thought. Such presence.

'Are you OK?' She saw a slight softening of the

mouth, a concern momentarily in the deep, dark eyes. 'You look a little pale.'

She nodded, conscious of a curious reaction at being addressed directly; exhilaration, rapture, a sudden surge of well-being that made absolutely no sense at all. He was. . .magnificent. 'Yes. . .yes, I'm fine,' she murmured. 'I just banged my cheek a little on contact, that's all.'

He walked slowly towards her, ignoring the taxi driver, who stood near by with his face set in an angry scowl. 'Where? Here?' Shockingly the man, the stranger, raised a hand and placed cool fingers to her face, touching the slightly reddened skin with a gentleness that completely disarmed. Olivia's pulse began an erratic beat. He smelt wonderful; a mixture of fresh cologne and suede jacket and fresh, clean skin. A perfect combination. A potential feast for all five of her senses.

'Looks as if there will be a slight bruise. Your face could end up being quite sore.' His touch lingered. 'If I were you I'd sue.'

'Now look here!'

More bluster from the taxi man, but Olivia wasn't listening, and neither, it seemed, was the stranger. Her eyes rested on the tanned throat, the curl of dark hair visible at the opening of the shirt, as he continued to make contact.

'What's your name?'

She tried to still the fluttering in her stomach as intense jet eyes lingered on her face. Feeling like this, juvenile, gauche, unable to identify a million and one other emotions, was unnerving to say the least. 'Olivia.' Her voice came out as little more than a squeak. She cleared her throat and tried again. 'Olivia Hamilton.'

'Jake Savage.' His hand fell from her cheek at last and was offered in a greeting that seemed totally natural, totally right, despite the absurdity of the situation. 'Pleased to meet you.' Olivia, sensing the dry humour in his tone, placed her own hand in his, briefly, silently. 'And you are?' He broke contact completely and the dark gaze switched direction, the tone hardening in an instant as the taxi driver was once again put under formidable scrutiny.

'Oh, no, mate!' The small man shook his head. 'No chance! This bang is your fault.' The taxi driver walked around to the front of his crumpled bonnet. 'Just look at this! I want *your* details, *your* name. This passenger's my witness. She'll tell you I wasn't driving too fast. Won't yer, love?'

A patronising arm was suddenly being wound possessively around her shoulders. Olivia extricated herself and took a few steps away from the stocky figure. She didn't see why she should lie to save him. It wasn't her way; never had been, never would be.

She took a steadying breath. 'I'm afraid,' she announced in a clear voice that bore no resemblance to the one she had used with Jake Savage, 'that I thought you were taking the bends too fast.' She glanced at the spiteful, angry face and decided to go on. 'And you certainly didn't keep to the speed limit when you went through the village.'

She was cursed immediately, the sharp words uttered with such unnecessary venom that Olivia stood shocked, her mouth sagging open a little at the abusive words used to describe her. She tried to think of something to say in return, but before she could utter a single word Jake Savage was gripping the denim shirt and the foul-mouthed taxi driver was being spun away, slammed forcibly against his own crumpled bonnet.

'Apologise to the lady!' The voice, low and controlled, was of a man used to being obeyed. Olivia watched in amazement as the taxi driver was lifted bodily by the lapels of his shirt and slammed back down on the car with a thud. There was a moment of tense, shocked silence. 'Go on!' Jake Savage's voice was as quietly menacing as his expression. 'Do it now before I'm tempted to knock that thick skull of yours off your pathetic little shoulders!'

A hastily muttered apology rang out in the dank, cold air. 'Now,' Jake Savage gave the man his freedom accompanied by a look of irritated disgust, 'get back in this pathetic heap of rust and get out of my sight before I do something that I might regret!'

Olivia stared down at her luggage, dumped unceremoniously in the middle of the road. It was extremely gloomy now. The dark rain clouds overhead were preparing to do their worst. 'You didn't get his name or insurance number,' she murmured, glancing back down the lane, her nostrils prickling at the smell of burning rubber.

'The logo of the firm he drives for was written all over the car—that will do.'

The reply was terse. Olivia raised her head, pushed back honey-coloured strands of hair from her eyes and looked straight into the disturbingly handsome face. 'Did you have to manhandle him like that?' she murmured, still unable to fully accept all that had happened. 'It. . .it was a little over the top, wasn't it?'

The firm mouth tightened into a line of disbelief.

Arrogant ebony eyes speared her face. 'You prefer being insulted by a goon?'

'He seemed pretty amenable before,' Olivia replied miserably, thinking about her futile hopes of a happy, trouble-free arrival. 'He was probably just tired. Or maybe he had money worries,' she added as an afterthought; 'perhaps he has a wife and any number of children to support and the accident was the last straw—'

'Stop making excuses for him! He was a foulmouthed bully and if you can't see that then you must be particularly stupid.'

Anger flared out of nowhere. Olivia narrowed her eyes and glared. 'It was your attitude that made him mad. I'm sure if you had handled it a little more tactfully. . .' There was a pause as he surveyed her. Olivia felt uncertainty growing under the withering gaze and discovered she didn't like this new phenomenon.

'I'm not prepared to waste my time arguing with you,' Jake Savage asserted with crisp authority. 'Now, where is it you are headed?' He pulled back the cuff of his jacket and glanced briefly at a silver Rolex. 'If it's not too far I may be able to give you a lift.'

'Just *may*?' Olivia drew herself up to her full five feet eight inches and altered her expression to match the formidable chill that was evident in the handsome features now. 'Here I am, stranded. . .in a strange place in the middle of nowhere, due largely to your macho shenanigans! And there's a possibility that you might leave me here, in the dark!'

'Macho shenanigans?' He looked faintly amused, which didn't help Olivia's temper any. 'What are you talking about? I didn't even raise my voice, let alone my fists. You were insulted, I defended you. Are you now saying you would have preferred it if I'd left well alone?'

Olivia worked hard at putting her executive persona to full use. There was no reason to allow this man to patronise her so effectively; she hadn't done anything wrong and she'd be damned if she'd allow him to talk to her as if she had! 'I can handle my own problems,' she asserted stiffly. 'I don't need other people fighting my battles for me!'

The lips curved into an infuriating, mocking smile and Olivia felt her irritation increase. 'In that case, I'll be on my way. I'll use my car phone and order you another taxi—or does that constitute too much help?'

Another taxi? Olivia's heart sank at the prospect. She watched miserably as Jake Savage strolled over to his Range Rover. 'I only have to go a mile or so along this lane,' she informed him stiffly.

He turned back towards her, raising a dark brow in query. 'Is that a request for a lift?'

Olivia scowled, infuriated with herself, with him, with the whole ridiculous situation. 'Yes.'

'Well, in that case,' ebony eyes lingered on her angry face and there was sudden amusement hovering near the corners of his mouth, 'how can I refuse?' He strolled back towards her and picked up a couple of Olivia's suitcases.

'Of course. . .I realise the accident wasn't your fault. . .and if you have somewhere to go. . .' she murmured, endeavouring to take the sting out of her voice and failing quite comprehensively, as he consulted his watch yet again. 'I don't want to disrupt your plans in any way. Maybe it would be best if I waited for another taxi.'

'You disrupted my plans when the taxi you were in collided with my vehicle,' he drawled with aggravating superiority, lifting up the back of the Range Rover to stow Olivia's luggage inside. 'It's a little late for apologies now.'

'I wasn't actually apologising!' she retorted sharply. 'It may or may not have come to your attention, but I wasn't actually driving the damned taxi!'

Jake Savage looked at her provokingly, his gaze traversing the length of her body with an infuriating lack of speed. 'I never said you were.'

Attraction and now anger. Before. . .when she had first set eyes on him a hundred and one ridiculous notions had gone through her head, none of which bore thinking about now. Too humiliating, each and every one of them. Images that had shocked and seduced. All of them totally insane, absolutely impossible. . .

Get a grip! she chided silently. You've encountered handsome, arrogant members of the male species before — there were thousands of them littered all over London, so why allow this one to affect you so badly?

'It wasn't actually my fault, you know!' Olivia repeated irritably. 'I was just the passenger, and besides, if you hadn't have gone over the top the way you did, with the heavy macho bit, I wouldn't have been stranded and you wouldn't have had to give me a lift in the first place.'

'I still don't.' Jake Savage turned and looked down at her with eyes that gleamed and an expression that told her to watch her step. He glanced overhead. 'It's about to rain. Do you think you could possibly stop talking and pass me up those last two suitcases? If we don't get a move-on we're both going to get very wet indeed.'

She was tempted to tell him what he could do with his lift. But that would mean her much longed-for new beginning would turn into even more of a disaster and there was no way she could manage all this luggage on her own. And he was right, she thought, glancing up at the sky; it was going to rain.

The deluge began just as the last of Olivia's luggage was packed in the Range Rover. The rear door was slammed shut with a curse and dark eyes speared her face. 'Well, what are you waiting for, permission? Go on, get in!' he ordered as Olivia attempted to shelter beneath the inadequate folds of her long cashmere cardigan.

The interior was all male; no lipsticks lying around, no boxes of tissues, no stray toys. He wasn't married, he didn't have a family, and if he had a woman, which he probably did, he didn't allow her to encroach on the day-to-day running of his life. Olivia, damp and breathless, told herself all this in a few seconds. Although why it should have been of any importance. . .

'What on earth have you got in the back there?' He climbed up and took his seat behind the wheel. 'The kitchen sink? You must be taking one hell of a long holiday.'

'It's not a holiday,' Olivia replied, averting her eyes from the strong profile beside her as she fastened her seat belt and tried to assume an aura of calm assurance. 'I've come to live here.'

He turned to look at her and Olivia, disarmed and disorientated by the direct gaze, smoothed her damp blonde hair back from her face and wondered what sort of a mess she looked.

'Just you and your suitcases?' There was derision again, and a hint of scorn evident in the rugged features, as if the prospect of Olivia settling amongst the local community was not realistic in some way. She was aware of the dark eyes sliding over her figure; her plum-coloured dress and matching cardigan had got more than a little damp and as his gaze lingered she felt as if the outfit was clinging to every contour.

'Yes!' she replied. 'Is there something wrong with that? Look, would you stop staring at me like that?' she snapped, unable to endure the steady, speculative gaze a moment longer. 'What's the matter, have I suddenly grown two heads or something?'

The impassive features didn't flicker, but then a predatory smile lifted the corners of the finely moulded mouth. 'No, you've still got just the one.' He turned the key in the ignition and the engine roared into life. 'Interesting,' he drawled, 'you don't like me looking at you.'

'Was I supposed to?' Olivia responded sharply.

'I was just returning the favour,' he informed her provokingly. 'You did seem to find it pretty difficult to drag your eyes away from my body earlier on.'

'Why, you—!'

'So,' he continued smoothly, cutting through Olivia's angry response, 'where exactly is it that I'm taking you?'

Olivia glanced across at the handsome face. To heaven—or to hell and back? she wondered. The words seared into her mind. She felt suddenly disorientated, shocked by the strength of her reactions to this man, bemused by the intense emotions he seemed to be able to conjure up inside her.

'Are you OK?'

His eyes scanned her face with thrilling intensity. Olivia looked away, pressing a hand to her flaming cheek. 'Let me see.' He reached towards her and tilted her chin. 'Yes, it's starting to look pretty sore. Did you bang your head hard?' he asked, gently twisting her towards him so that he could look into her face.

'No. . .just my cheek. It wasn't much,' Olivia added swiftly. Did he think she was injured, concussed? Maybe she was, maybe that was why she felt so strange. 'I'm fine, honestly.'

'Do you have a headache?' She shook her head, azure eyes fixed helplessly now on the strong, rugged features. 'Does your neck hurt?' His hands slid down and she felt his fingers beneath the collar of her dress, pressing gently against her skin. 'Any pain there?'

'No.' She gulped an unsteady breath. 'I've told you. . . I'm all right.'

Ebony eyes narrowed. 'You don't look all right.'

Silence. A second passed, then ten. The rain was beating on the roof of the vehicle, but she didn't hear it—neither, it seemed, did he. She saw his look change, recognised the stunned awareness in his face so easily—it was as if she were looking into a mirror, as if he suddenly felt the same way as she. . .

'Olivia Hamilton.' Her name was like honey on his tongue. She watched, her clear blue eyes wide with wonder, hardly daring to think about what might happen next. He was moving closer, lowering his head with obvious intent. Olivia found her eyes transfixed on his mouth. Would he kiss her? *Would* he?

The insistent bleep of the car phone shattered the moment. Olivia gasped a breath and saw amazement flicker momentarily across Jake Savage's sharply angled features. He released her head and picked up the receiver, looking out through the windscreen into the darkening afternoon. 'Yes?'

There was a short conversation, but Olivia was hardly aware of what was said.

She glanced across at the strong profile and saw that the phone had been replaced and that he was speaking to her. 'Where to?'

'It's. . .not far from here. Just a mile or so along this road, as I said,' she informed him slowly. The dark eyes were looking at the road ahead now and she was able to feel more composed. 'There's a turning off to the left. You can't see that much of the cottage from the road, but it backs onto fields. There's a stream and a public footpath which runs near by and both lead directly into the village.' She was gabbling, and that was unlike her. She took a steadying breath. 'It's called—'

'I know what it's called. Honeysuckle Cottage.'

She tried to ignore the challenge in his eyes, but it was too strong, too infuriating. 'So you live near?' The question was out of her mouth before she could stop it.

He threw her an enigmatic look. 'Not far.'

'In the village?'

He looked at her thoughtfully for a moment. 'Not in the village, no. I have a place a couple of miles from here.' There was a slight pause. 'So, you've decided to buy this quaint little cottage.' He surveyed her with a curious expression. 'I wonder why.'

His direct gaze unsettled her, but she fought hard and managed not to let that fact show. 'I felt like a change.'

'Some change.'

A silence fell. Olivia looked down at her lap and wondered again if she had made the worst, most foolish decision of her entire life. Hell! What if she had? No job. No friends. She thought of the winter; cold and isolated and desolate.

'A penny for them? Or are highly paid executives' thoughts worth far more?'

Olivia glanced up and cursed silently; how did he know the sort of life she had led? Why couldn't that stupid taxi driver have driven more carefully? Why had she ever had to meet this man? 'There's no need to mock!' she retorted. 'Are you always this infuriating?'

'Not often. In fact, I can't think of the last time I was so tempted. It's been months...years,' he added quietly.

'Well, do you think you could cease laughing at my expense?' Olivia snapped. 'I'm not in the mood.'

'It's been quite a day, I should imagine.' Dark eyes speared her face. 'A shock to the system,' he murmured softly.

Olivia felt the hairs on the back of her neck stand up on end. His eyes. His voice. She felt a lurch of awareness kick her in the stomach and worked hard at trying to ignore it. Such a desperately attractive voice. He knew it, of course; men like him always did. 'I'm looking forward to my new life,' she declared resolutely. 'There are masses of things I plan to do!'

'Such as?'

She wouldn't tell him. Her ideas for using part of the orchard as a tea garden, and converting one of the outside sheds into a bric-à-brac-cum-junk shop were still only in the early planning stages. He would probably shoot the whole lot down in flames with some clever remark and she didn't want that—not whilst she was feeling so fragile, anyway. 'Oh, all sorts of things,' she murmured vaguely. 'Once the cottage is how I want it, I'll be able to view all of my options.'

'Does one of those options include finding a job?' Jake enquired. 'Or are you wealthy enough not to have to worry about that sort of thing?'

'I'll be OK for a while. Look, I did know what I was letting myself in for,' Olivia added, noting the disbelief in his expression. 'I made this decision. My reasons are sound and. . .and it's going to work!'

'Who are you trying to convince?' he drawled. 'So you've left London, in something of a hurry, I would say, and you're here all alone out in the sticks.'

'Yes. How. . .do you know that?'

Dark eyes surveyed the long, richly coloured woollen clothes, the large gilt bangle that hung from her right wrist, the expensive rings and professionally styled hair.

'You've got that city look; a pallor that stems from too many hours spent in an air-conditioned office. The superficial gloss from a superficial life,' he drawled. 'Let's just say us country folk can spot it a mile off.'

'Well, congratulations on your perception, Mr Savage, but surely it takes one to know one—I can't say I see a great deal of the country yokel about you!' Olivia retorted angrily.

'I hide it well.' He swung the Range Rover around a bend and then took a turning on the right, which led to a tree-lined lane.

Another terse reply. Olivia scowled. God! How she hated arrogant, egotistical males!

'What exactly did you do in London?'

They were pulling into the driveway now. Olivia pressed the switch for the electric window and felt a surge of excitement rising as she looked at her new home. 'I was in publishing,' she murmured, narrowing her eyes against the rain that spat in at her face.

'And you left? Why?'

'I don't actually see that it's any of your business?' Olivia flashed.

He shrugged. 'For some peculiar reason I find myself interested—isn't that enough?'

Olivia forced a sweet smile that dripped with sarcasm. It was a famous weapon. At work she had been renowned for it. 'Surprisingly, Mr Savage, no it is not!' No effect. Olivia exhaled an impatient breath. 'I happen to be a private and—'

'Independent woman,' he finished drily.

Olivia nodded, satisfied that he was at last getting the picture. 'That's right.'

'I would hazard a guess and say that that last quality is extremely important to you,' he murmured, watching her resolute expression. 'Am I right?'

'Of course! Independence and freedom of choice—the most important things anyone can ever possess!' she declared with absolute authority.

'You really think so?'

Olivia showed her surprise. 'Don't you?'

He shrugged. 'Maybe.'

'Just maybe?' Olivia queried. 'Only that?'

The attractive mouth twisted into a grim smile. 'Freedom of choice—it's not always the easiest of things to acquire.'

Olivia's well-shaped brows drew together in query. 'Isn't it? Somehow I can't imagine you ever having difficulty in that department!' she responded tartly. '*I* would hazard a guess and say in your case that precious commodity money is not in short supply.'

'You believe it all comes down to personal finance?'

Olivia glanced up at the glittering gaze, conscious once more of the derisive edge in his voice. What had she said? Why did he look so aggravated all of a

sudden? 'That has a lot to do with it,' she murmured.
'Well, yes, I do, as a matter of fact!' she added, refusing
to be put off by the disapproving vibes that were
suddenly emanating from the powerful frame, determined to be perverse. 'Money brings choice. There's
no question about that. Look,' she added, angered by
the now blatant look of steely dislike, 'I was ambitious.
I worked myself into the ground for eight years, made
it to the top. I enjoyed the work, I was powerful, in my
own small sphere, but the only solid thing I've got to
show for it, the only thing that matters at the end of all
that hard slog is the fact that I have a healthy bank
balance and some good investments. Money brought
me here,' she added firmly, 'it brought me this change
of lifestyle, this pretty cottage in the country. The
ability to choose.'

There was a strange, almost dangerous silence. 'And
what if choice is restrained by other limitations, other
boundaries? What if you can't bring yourself to just
walk away? What then?'

Olivia frowned. This conversation was getting deep.
She wasn't sure she could handle it. . .she wasn't sure
she *wanted* to. 'I. . .don't understand,' she murmured,
playing dumb. 'I don't know what you're talking about.'

'Oh, I think you do,' he murmured softly. 'But it's
easier. . .you prefer to see things clearly—black and
white; that's right, isn't it? No grey areas allowed?'

'I try to.' Olivia paused to consider and realised that
this man, who was a virtual stranger, was far too
perceptive for comfort. 'It makes decisions a lot easier.'

Dark brows drew together. 'Life isn't always that
simple, though, is it?'

Olivia hesitated and thought of Paul. 'You can make
it simple,' she declared forcibly. 'You can *choose* to

make it simple.' She saw the dark head shake in disbelief. 'Obviously we see things differently,' she declared. 'I'm not trying to convert you. You were the one who pursued this line of conversation!'

He glanced across at her. 'You're nervous—why?'

Olivia lifted her head and stared defiantly at the assured, handsome face. 'I'm. . .' She had been about to deny it—pointlessly, of course, because they both knew she was as nervous as hell. But of what? That was the point. And why? 'I. . .don't know you.' She shrugged awkwardly. 'And yet I find myself drawn into deep conversations that. . .that disturb me. . .and. . .' She closed her mouth abruptly and looked out of the car window. Honesty was falling out of her mouth at an alarming rate. What on earth had possessed her to be so frank. . .and to a perfect stranger?

'And?'

'It doesn't matter.' She lifted her head and glanced towards her new home. She took a deep breath and savoured the smell of the chill, damp air. This was it, the moment she had been dreaming about for weeks. 'Honeysuckle Cottage—it's a pretty name, isn't it?'

The harsh mouth curved suddenly. 'If you say so. Although there hasn't been a strand of the stuff growing there in all the years I can remember.'

Olivia removed her gaze from the arresting profile and watched the windscreen wipers moving back and forth. 'I'll grow some,' she announced.

'You feel like giving it a try?'

The mocking tone wasn't lost on her. Olivia looked sharply at the derisive mouth. 'Is there something wrong with that?' she demanded.

'It deserves to be lived in for fifty-two weeks of the year, not just now and then when the flat in London needs decorating, or the weather's fine,' he remarked sharply.

Olivia turned briefly, a frown creasing her forehead. 'I haven't got a flat in London, not any more,' she replied, registering the sharp disapproval of her companion's face, 'and even if I had, what business is it of yours how I live my life?'

She wrenched open the door as soon as the vehicle came to a halt and jumped down onto the crunchy gravel, conscious that she was in danger of allowing this disturbing man to mar the arrival she had so longed for. 'Thanks for the lift,' she continued stonily, rummaging in her roomy leather bag for the key. 'If you'll just open the back for me I'll get my luggage and you can go.'

'Here, take this.' He reached into the back seat of the vehicle and tossed a large grey raincoat through the open doorway. 'That wonderful but totally impractical dress is going to be ruined.' He got out and walked around to the boot. 'Go and open up and I'll start bringing your luggage inside.'

'There's absolutely no need—!'

He halted her protestations with a look. 'Go on! Do as I say! I was late before; I'm even later now. A couple more minutes of my time won't make a lot of difference.'

She complied. For one thing it was too wet to stand outside arguing the toss over whether he should or should not carry her bags, and for another they were heavy and there were a lot of them and she would definitely ruin her outfit in the process.

Olivia ran for the front door. The wooden gate creaked a little as she opened it. Her soft black leather boots brushed against clumps of newly sprouted foliage, which she promised herself she would one day recognise, as she negotiated the narrow overgrown path.

The cottage had been empty for a little while now. Out of the corner of her eye she spotted drifts of blue forget-me-nots and pale yellow primroses and her heart lifted and soared because there were so many days ahead and so much to do.

There was a porch overhead, but it was in need of repair and too old and rickety to afford much shelter from the torrential rain. Dragging her gaze away from the front garden, Olivia thrust her treasured key into the lock and stepped across the threshold into her new home.

It was dark inside. The rain clouds had hastened the spring afternoon towards evening. Olivia searched blindly for a light switch and, unable to find one near the door, groped her way across the room, banging into unidentifiable objects on the way. There had been a few pieces of furniture here when she had last visited; old stuff that would have to be thrown out. Olivia added another job to the list she carried around inside her head as she tried to make her way towards the kitchen; order a skip to cart away all this rubbish, so that the decorators could get started as soon as possible.

Her foot scuffed into something soft, an unseen object on the floor that nearly sent her flying into the wall. Olivia grabbed hold of the back of a nearby chair and turned around to take another look. What was it? An old carpet? Olivia let out a sigh of disgust. For goodness' sake! There had definitely been no carpet or rug here when she had visited before, she was sure of it. What a cheek!

'People dumping their rubbish here!' she muttered crossly, giving the object an irritated push with her foot.

It felt strange. Not a carpet or a rug. A prickle of alarm ran across Olivia's skin. She took a deep breath and bent down to try to get a better look. Oh, goodness! What was it? Slowly, very slowly she reached out a hand, forcing herself to be brave. It would be a lot better if she could see more; this was like that awful game she had played at a party once, where you had to stick your hand into a bag and feel and try to gess whatever was inside.

Her fingers reached out gingerly and came into hesitant contact with something that felt disgusting; a mixture of fur and a wet, sticky slime.

Olivia gave a shriek, jumped up and half stumbled, half ran for the front door.

She cannoned into Jake Savage, overloaded with cases at the entrance, and clutched onto the lapels of his jacket.

'Hey! What on earth's the matter?'

Olivia closed her eyes and allowed herself the brief pleasure of pressing her face against the soft suede jacket. 'There's something. . .something horrible in there,' she declared unsteadily, aware of her heart racing fit to burst, unsure whether it was entirely due to her sudden fright or the fact that she was in such close proximity to Jake Savage.

'What sort of thing?'

'I. . . I don't know. It's so dark and I can't find the damn light switch, but—'

'It's frightened the hell out of you,' he finished for her. His voice was calm. 'Funny how appearances can be so deceptive, isn't it?' he murmured softly. She could feel the masculine hardness of his body, the warmth of his breath on her face. 'Now what on earth made me imagine that the sophisticated Miss Hamilton could handle any situation, no matter how daunting? You're shaking like a leaf!'

'I. . . I don't like the dark very much,' Olivia admitted unsteadily. 'But it's not just that; there really is something horrible. I don't know what it is, but it felt absolutely disgusting!'

'OK, calm down.' The deep voice was soothing and immensely reassuring. 'I'm here.' Olivia heard the suitcases fall to the floor and her heart increased its hammering tenfold as she felt the pressure of strong masculine arms around her shoulders. 'There's no need to panic.' Firm fingers moved sensuously in a circular motion. 'I can still feel your whole body trembling, do you know that?' His voice trailed to a halt and Olivia sensed the change in him, so that when he spoke again it was no surprise to hear a softer, more intimate note to his voice. 'Such a fiery character on the outside. . .' he lifted a hand and tilted Olivia's chin so that he could look down into her face '. . .but not quite so hard on the inside, eh?'

Their souls met and the feeling of knowing assailed Olivia once again. She didn't understand what was happening, why she should feel this way about a man she had only just met.

She wanted him. Shock coursed through her body at the revelation and Olivia pulled away jerkily. 'Do you think you could. . .take a look?'

Jake released her without a word, she heard a reassuring flick and instantly the room was bathed in the glare of a naked bulb. They were in a large, pleasantly shaped room. Low beams criss-crossed the ceiling; a big inglenook fireplace dominated one whole wall. Olivia swallowed and forced herself to get a grip, self-consciously taking several large steps away from Jake Savage's broad frame. 'It was over there,' she murmured, hardly daring to meet the probing gaze, 'behind that old sofa.'

She stayed by the door, watching as he crossed to the place she had indicated. There was a sharp intake of breath and then a sigh. 'It's OK, nothing to be frightened of.' He pushed the sofa out of the way and Olivia tentatively moved forward. 'Just a battered, bruised and half-starved mutt.' Jake crouched down and placed seemingly knowledgeable hands onto the matted, blood-smeared fur. 'Which, surprisingly, is still alive!' There was a note of triumph in the deep tone. He turned suddenly and she saw the expression of urgency that accompanied it. 'Hurry! Run out to my car and grab the black case that's on the back seat.'

'Right!' Olivia wheeled around, not pausing to question or consider his order. She gripped his raincoat around her shoulders, dashed out into the pouring rain and returned in less than half a minute with the large black case as requested.

'You're a doctor?' She couldn't keep the note of surprise from her voice as she watched Jake flick open the case and pull out a stethoscope.

'Vet.' He nodded towards the unmoving, furry mass. 'Pretty fortunate dog, huh?'

Olivia frowned, her eyes switching to the miserable-looking animal on the floor. 'It doesn't look very fortunate. You honestly think you can save it?'

He didn't answer immediately. There was silence and immense concentration as he listened to the dog's heartbeat. Finally he lifted his head. 'Looks hopeful.

There's a reasonable beat, considering the state he's in. He's weak from lack of food, of course, and there are a couple of bad gashes.' Jake carefully lifted a back leg and examined a septic-looking wound. 'This one is pretty nasty. Stopped him from finding anything to eat in the last few days, I should think.'

'But he looks so. . .so desperate,' Olivia replied, gritting her teeth as a needle was swiftly filled and injected into the mangy body. 'How do you think he came to be here?'

Jake lifted his broad shoulders in a shrug. 'Who knows? Maybe he slipped in when your things were being delivered earlier.' He glanced towards a couple of packing cases that were in the corner of the room. 'I need some water, hot water. Can you see to it?'

Olivia straightened up, aware of the professional command in his voice. 'Yes.'

'Good.' He began to roll up his shirt-sleeves and Olivia, despite her determined resolution to be as efficient as possible, found her gaze drawn to the powerful forearms, the strength of his hands as they lowered to examine the dog. 'Are you going to get that hot water now,' he enquired sharply as the seconds passed, 'or do I have to get it myself?'

She turned quickly, cursing her wandering concentration, cursing the fact that this man could make her feel wonderful one moment and totally inadequate the next, with no more than a look and a few crisply spoken words.

By the time she came back into the living-room with a bowl full of warm water, another with hot water in it, a towel and some soap, determined to be Miss Efficiency, Jake had carried the dog over to the sofa. She watched as he clipped away sodden black fur from around several different wounds.

'I don't suppose there's any chance of you lighting a fire, is there?' Dark eyes flicked across to the large, blackened inglenook fireplace. 'Only it's pretty cold in here and this dog needs all the warmth he can get.'

Olivia shivered; her own woollen dress felt decidedly damp from the rain and she was having to grit her teeth to stop them chattering together as it was. 'I'm not very organised,' she murmured, frowning at the fireplace. 'There isn't any wood or anything yet. I was going to get that kind of thing sorted out tomorrow.' She paused, glad that she didn't have to admit that she had never lit an open fire in her life before. 'But I do have a couple of fan heaters. I bought them specially for the move. They should be in a case upstairs. I'll go get them.'

The room felt a lot warmer after half an hour or so, not cosy exactly but better than when they had first entered. Olivia had found a couple of bulbs for the wall lights and retrieved a large rectangular rug from one of the packing cases, which she had spread over the bare boards. The dog had been encouraged to eat a special nourishing concoction that had been mixed from a selection of packets carried in the Range Rover.

'Right. That's just about all I can do for now.' Jake Savage flexed his broad shoulders and released a long-drawn-out breath. 'Don't worry, he looks a lot worse than he is; he's going to be fine,' he added, seeing Olivia's anxious gaze. 'He just needs rest and a lot of feeding up now, and daily attention to his wounds, of course. They should heal well, though; he's a young dog and there's no reason why he shouldn't make a swift recovery.'

Olivia smiled her relief. 'That's good.' She glanced down at the sleeping animal. 'Would you. . .like a cup of tea before you go?' Olivia made her voice sound as casual as possible, and she glanced up into Jake Savage's face. He looked tired; it crossed her mind that maybe he hadn't been sleeping well lately. 'I realise you've stayed far longer than you wanted to, but the kettle's just boiled, so. . .'

There was a slight pause and then the lips curled into a brief, unexpected smile. 'That would be good—thank you. I take mine white, no sugar.'

Olivia released a cautious breath and found that relief was flooding through her. Jake Savage had been tending to the dog for almost an hour and in that time she had become increasingly anxious that once his task was at an end he would pick up his bag and the animal and walk out of her life without another word.

*Why*? The question raced into her mind. Why did it matter that she might not see him again?

He stood up, rubbing the back of his neck in a gesture that communicated a deeply ingrained tiredness, unthinkingly stretching to his full height of six feet plus, and immediately cracking his head against one of the low blackened beams.

'Oh, my goodness! Are you OK?' Olivia winced at the sound of his skull meeting oak and rushed towards him, frowning in sympathy, instinctively reaching up and touching the dark, glossy head. 'This ceiling is dreadfully low, isn't it? You'll have to be careful in future.'

She stilled, her whole being transfixed by the feel of his thick black hair beneath her fingers, by the close proximity of Jake Savage's powerful body, by her words. She was overwhelmingly conscious of what she

had just said—the *future*? Did she think they had one?
Did she imagine she would see this man again after
today? Did she want to?

She tried to snatch her hand away, but Jake Savage
was far too swift for her. 'It's just here,' he murmured.
His large hand covered hers, moving her fingers across
his head. Dark, dangerous eyes looked down into her
face. 'Can you feel that?'

Olivia's fingers came into contact with a raised bump
and she nodded. 'Y. . .yes.' Physical contact with this
man meant she was whispering again, as if the effect of
touching or being touched by him somehow diminished
the power of her vocal cords. 'It must hurt,' she
murmured, wishing she had the strength to pull her
fingers free, knowing deep down that she didn't want
to.

His gaze was intense, focusing steadily on her
increasingly mobile expression.

Olivia swallowed. A stillness settled over the interior
of the room. He didn't speak. He didn't have to. There
was no confusing this sensation of inevitability. Olivia
ran her tongue nervously over her parched lips and
waited, catching her breath a little as the dark head
lowered very slowly, very deliberately.

This was what she had been waiting for all of her
life. She hadn't been wrong before.

This man called Jake Savage would mean something
to her, meeting him, wanting him, loving him.

This was her destiny.

# CHAPTER TWO

JAKE claimed her whole being with a passionate, sensual kiss that caused Olivia's world to tilt on its axis. His mouth was warm and sensual and searching. Her lips parted of their own accord and she felt the true taste of him, she felt the energy, the longing, the need burning between them. . .

No words were necessary. What was there to say? The electricity, the unexplainable certainty that this would happen, had been between them from the beginning. Since that first look, that first touch. . .

His hands were impatient. Searching, moving sensually over the close-fitting dress, exploring every outline, every curve. She gasped as he dragged his mouth from her lips and began kissing the arched curve of her neck, pulling back her cardigan from her shoulders to reveal the covered zip of her dress.

Olivia's hands flew to his shirt, twisting, gripping the fabric. She felt as if she were drowning and only this man could save her. Trembling fingers slipped beneath the fabric and she felt for the first time the true power of his frame, the strength of pure muscle, the softness of tanned skin, the roughness of dark, curling hair. She felt, too, his reaction to her touch, the sharp breath, the increased pressure of his mouth on her lips.

It was the swift intensity that affected her so deeply. She wanted, shockingly, to be free of the restriction of her clothes. She wanted, she *ached* to feel the roughness of his hands on her naked body. . .

He knew. Men like Jake Savage always knew.

She gasped as his fingers grazed her skin. Feelings Olivia didn't even know she possessed spun wildly around inside her head as he began to unfasten her dress. This passion that had been there, lying between them from the beginning, needed assuaging, it needed to reach the ultimate climax. No time to talk, no time to get to know one another—that could come later. . .

'My bedroom. . .upstairs.' Her voice was a whisper. A great part of her could hardly believe she was daring to be so bold. Cool, prim Olivia Hamilton? 'Frigid Olivia', as Paul had once described her?

'Has it a bed?' His voice was deep and husky, his mouth warm and hungry against her skin.

'Of course.' She raised her head and kissed him passionately, pressing her body against his towering frame. 'At least, I hope so. . .'

'In that case. . .' Jake swung her into his arms as if she weighed no more than a feather and carried her effortlessly up the narrow staircase.

His tread sounded hollow on the bare boards and as he carried her in the darkness Olivia knew a fleeting moment of doubt.

He dragged his mouth from hers, pausing on the top step, sensing the sudden rigidity of her slim frame. 'You do *want* this. . .?' Silvery moonlight shone through the landing window, illuminating the rugged planes of his face. 'Olivia?' His dark eyes were questioning.

She looked up at him, her eyes scanning every angle, every contour of his face. She knew what she wanted. Rational thought tried to spoil the way she felt, but she thrust it away. Why should she follow her old rules? *Why should she*? She ached with wanting him. Never before had she experienced such passionate need, such desperate, intense longing.

'Yes,' she murmured unsteadily. 'Yes, I do.'

She clung to him as he caressed her body, gasping with pleasure as his powerful hands took control. Waiting for the right moment. . .wanting her first experience to mean something, to be special. . . All those months of rebuffing Paul's impatient advances. . . it had all been justified. She had waited for this moment, this *man* for all of her life.

He took sudden and full possession of her then and Olivia found herself crying aloud, tensing a little in spite of everything.

'Olivia?' She heard the ragged incredulity in his voice, the sharp intake of breath as Jake fought his own physical needs and desires. 'You're a—!'

'Please!' Olivia whispered imploringly, acutely aware that her world would fall apart if he rejected her now. 'It's all right.' She gripped his body tightly, moved against him, pressed her lips against the bronzed skin of his shoulder, working to convince him anyway she knew how. 'I want this!'

There was a split-second of hesitation, then a faint groan as will-power vanished. 'So do I,' he confessed, his voice gruff with desire, 'so do I. . .'

He was a magnificent lover. Better than Olivia had imagined even in her wildest dreams; strong and power-ful, ruthlessly in control, but with kisses that were tender as well as passionate, a touch that possessed silk as well as steel. . .

Olivia found herself crying aloud many times, but there was no pain involved once that special moment had been passed. Only pleasure—pleasure for them both.

It took some time for their desire to diminish; they made love, they kissed and touched and then they wanted each other again. The evening slipped into night and eventually their passion was satisfied.

In the darkness Olivia could hear Jake's ragged breathing. She felt replete, wonderful, oozing with a happiness that she didn't wish to analyse.

And Jake?

Olivia moved to look at him. Her head had been resting on the firm, hard chest, but as she moved so did he, lifting her from him, slipping away from her, accompanied by a sharp, almost angry release of breath until there was no longer any physical contact.

'Jake?' Olivia's voice was tentative, uncertain in the half-light. She reached across and cautiously touched the muscular hair-roughened arm that lay a distance from hers. 'Jake?'

'Yes?' His tone was enigmatic, flat almost. Olivia felt the sharp stab of rejection, like a knife through her body. What had she expected? A declaration of love? Some word that would indicate he felt as moved as she?

Destiny. The word reverberated in her mind. They were meant to be lovers. She knew it. She felt it with her whole being. This had not been a mistake. Knowing it filled her mind. The future stretched ahead, bright and full of meaning now that she had met this man.

But she didn't like this silence; it frightened her.

A shaft of despair ran through Olivia's body. Surely he wasn't regretting all that had just taken place? Surely not. 'It. . .it was OK, wasn't it?'

'Yes.'

Olivia swallowed and closed her eyes. What was wrong? Why was he being so. . .so distant? She felt movement beside her and saw in the half-light that he had raised himself to a sitting position.

'It was more than OK,' he asserted roughly, as if the admission was being dragged out of him. 'You know that.'

'Do I?' She sounded like a child; young and immensely vulnerable.

'The seduction. . .' There was a pause. She could feel him searching for words in the darkness. 'It wasn't planned, it wasn't premeditated. . .' His voice was deep, rough-edged. 'I don't want you to think that I wander the countryside seducing lone women! It took me as much by surprise as it did you.'

'I know that,' Olivia replied unsteadily, watching his outline as he dragged strong fingers through sweat-slicked hair. He sounded bewildered, as if already regretting his indulgence in the pleasures of the flesh.

'How do you know?' He looked down at her, silvery moonlight flashing like steel in his eyes. 'We've just met, Olivia, remember?' he reminded her unsteadily. 'You know as little about me as I do about you! You were a virgin, for God's sake!' He flung the word at her like an accusation. 'Why didn't you tell me?'

'It didn't seem important,' Olivia replied quietly.

'Not *important*?'

'You know what I mean!' Olivia hated the way he was making her feel. She tried desperately to find the right words that would make him understand. 'I wanted you to make love to me.'

She heard him release a taut breath. 'I know.'

Olivia tried to swallow but her throat felt tight. She shivered in the chill room. 'You're regretting what's happened, aren't you?'

'No.' His voice was flat. He looked across at Olivia

and she felt rather than saw the intensity of his gaze. 'How could I regret any of what's just taken place?' he added quietly. 'But we're strangers. . .'

Was that all it was? Olivia felt a sense of relief wash over her. 'We could change that,' she replied simply.

'What?'

Was he being deliberately cruel? His voice sounded harsh and scornful suddenly, amazed, outraged even, as if she had suggested something dreadful. Surely not. Jake had been so sensitive, so caring during their lovemaking.

Everything was going wrong. Tears welled in Olivia's eyes and she shut them tight, glad of the virtual darkness of the room. 'I just thought—'

'Well, don't!' He released a heavy sigh. 'Please, don't think! Look, Olivia. It was good. Hell, it was better than good, but don't go getting the wrong idea.' Jake reached over and for a fleeting moment she felt the warmth of his touch on her face. 'I don't regret what's taken place between us, I've told you that, but I'm not interested in involvement, or emotional ties or anything that even remotely resembles a relationship.' He released a taut breath and swung away from her. 'So if you're under the illusion that—'

'I'm not!' Olivia's voice was sharp. She was having to think fast and talk even faster. Such *humiliation*! She could hardly bear it. She had given this man everything. She had followed her true feelings, been guided by the deepest of emotions, only to have it all thrown back in her face. She hardened her voice. 'You've obviously got the wrong impression. Don't worry, Jake, I'm not the clinging type!'

She heard a relieved breath. 'Good.' There was an

agonising pause. 'Look,' he continued eventually, 'if I've made you feel bad or cheated then I'm sorry—'

Pain twisted like a knife in a wound. She didn't want his sympathy! 'You haven't!' Olivia took a steadying breath and continued determinedly, 'I've come to this part of the world to be free from ties and complications. I've just. . .extracted myself from a rather messy emotional tangle and the last thing I want is another relationship! I'm. . . I'm just not interested.'

'So we feel the same way?' His voice was cool, but questioning, and she could sense the importance attached to the enquiry.

Olivia gulped a breath and swung her legs off the bed, groping for her clothes, feeling the damp wool of her dress beneath her fingers. 'It would seem so. Now,' she made an effort and hardened her voice still further, 'I think it's best if you go.' She attempted a short laugh that sounded strained and unnatural in the gloom. 'After all, I'm hardly in a position to offer much in the way of hospitality, am I? The place is a mess and it's freezing up here!'

'You'll be all right?' His voice momentarily held concern in the darkness of the bedroom. 'If you want help with anything—'

Olivia swung back round to glare at the large, formidable outline. 'Just go, will you?' she gritted. 'It's been a long day. I'm tired and I'm cold and now that it's all over and we know where we both stand I just want you out of my house!'

'As you wish.' The warmth in Jake's voice had turned to ice. He rose from the bed and picked up his clothes from the floor. Olivia watched, tears glistening in her eyes, as he dressed without haste. She couldn't remember the last time she had felt so desolate, so alone.

'I suppose...' Olivia cleared her throat and tried to stop herself from shivering '...there's a girlfriend waiting for you somewhere?' She held her breath and then forced herself to say it. 'A wife?'

'There's no one.' His voice was terse, almost savage. 'I thought I'd just made that clear! I'm no adulterer! I'm simply not interested in any long-term relationship.' He finished fastening his shirt and looked across towards the bed. 'I've already been taught my lesson. I'd be a fool not to learn from it.' There was a slight pause. 'You must be cold,' he murmured. 'I'll bring up a couple of your suitcases.'

'There's no need!'

'Yes, there is. Your dress was damp from the storm—you can't put that on again.'

'I told you not to bother!' Olivia snapped as he walked out of the bedroom. 'I don't need kindness,' she called wildly. 'I don't need you treating me like a child...or one of your damn animals!' she added as an afterthought.

No reply. It was worse than an argument. Suddenly she wanted to fight him. Suddenly she hated him. Why didn't he feel the same way as she did? How could she have made such a dreadful mistake?

Whilst he was gone Olivia sprang from the bed and struggled with her underclothes. She felt so vulnerable. So foolish. She heard his footsteps on the stairs and fumbled wildly with the catch of her bra.

'Here. Your clothes.' Jake dumped a suitcase onto the bed and flicked on the light.

'I want you to go!'

'I will. But not before you've found something to wear.' He clicked open one of the cases and glanced across, dark eyes resting impassively on Olivia's half-naked figure. 'Do you want some help with that?'

'It's OK, I can manage.'

'It's twisted.'

'I can manage.'

He wasn't listening. Jake walked towards her and Olivia took a few steps back. 'What's the matter?' He looked fierce. His mouth tightened ominously as Olivia shook her head.

'Just go!'

'I will once you stop looking so petrified. Now turn around and let me help you.'

'Don't touch me!'

'Don't be ridiculous,' he replied calmly, 'We've just made love. I've done more than touch you!'

'I wish to God you hadn't!'

She felt his fingers still and her heart stopped beating. He was so close. His black hair was still tousled from their lovemaking and Olivia had to beat down the desire to reach up a hand and smooth it into place.

'You don't mean that.' Cool authority masked his anger as he looked down into her face.

Olivia's bottom lip trembled, but she bit down on it and stared up fiercely, her wide blue eyes clashing with Jake Savage's formidable gaze. 'Don't I?'

'You were more passionate than any woman I've made love to,' he asserted quietly, touching her cheek briefly with his hand. 'Don't spoil it all now by lying!'

'Spoil it?' Olivia released an unsteady breath. '*You* can say that to *me*?'

'I don't make promises I can't keep!' he informed her tersely. 'I don't lie, I don't deceive. I'm not a damned hypocrite!' His expression was taut suddenly, a cold, metallic mask that froze her very soul. 'Believe me, over the years I've seen enough hypocrisy to last me a lifetime! We made love this evening because it felt like the thing to do. Because it was the *only* thing to do!'

'Please!' Olivia cried desperately. 'Can't you understand that I regret everything that's just taken place?'

He looked at her with a frown. 'And you honestly expect me to believe that?' The dark head shook with disbelief. 'OK. I'll go,' he murmured. 'But don't imagine this is the end—'

'I want it to be!'

Jake's mouth curved slightly. 'No, you don't.' Dark eyes slid over her bare breasts. He reached forward and stroked a darkened nipple with one finger and Olivia felt the now familiar ache of desire his touch could produce all over again. 'What we achieved tonight is rare,' he asserted knowledgeably. 'Neither of us could deny ourselves the pleasure of such sexual harmony. It has to continue.'

Words failed her. Olivia opened her mouth to speak, to deny all that he said, but nothing emerged. 'You see?' Jake was observing her reactions closely. 'You know deep down that what I say is the truth.' He slid his fingers across her breast and adjusted the strap of her bra. 'I'll let myself out.'

She watched him leave the room, rigid with resentment, shocked by what he had said. Did he really imagine that she would be willing to. . .to. . .continue after all that had just been said?

There was a biting wind outside that howled mournfully through the trees. Olivia drew back the faded bedroom curtains and felt the sharp breeze blowing into the room through the old, ill-fitting windows.

She shivered, watching silently as Jake placed the

sedated dog carefully inside the back of the Range Rover and then covered it with a tartan blanket. There was a brief glow as the interior light went on, a glimpse of Jake Savage's hard, enigmatic expression. Then darkness, the roar of a powerful engine, a glow of red tail-lights and in the next moment the Range Rover was pulling away into the night.

Next morning it was still raining. Olivia stood at her bedroom window and stared across the fields, watching impassively as the low clouds drifted in sheets of grey.

April showers, she thought. Except that today was the first day of May, and this definitely was no shower. She glanced around the attic-style bedroom and considered going back to bed. It was early yet, not even seven o'clock, and it was cold and dismal. . .

He was on her mind, of course. She had dreamt about him in the early hours of the morning; a re-enacting of their lovemaking the previous night.

Olivia wrapped her dressing-gown tightly around her and longed for central heating. Amendment to the list, she thought; get a heating firm to install an efficient system as soon as possible — wood fires in every room were not going to be possible or practical.

He had left his jacket. It was the first thing her eyes alighted on when she came downstairs. She picked up the expensive suede garment and looked at it for a long while, her mind swinging back to the previous evening, to the shock and pleasure of his embrace. Her body stirred at the memory. The intensity; that had been the thing that had lingered on far into the night, still lingered even now. How could he have told her he wasn't interested in involvement after making love to her like that?

The jacket felt soft beneath her fingers; she saw that it was a little worn at the cuffs and guessed instinctively that it was a favoured article.

Olivia pressed her face against the suede and breathed in the unforgettable scent of him. Smell was important to her; in London the toxic fumes of the street, the impersonal, clinical smell of her hi-tech office had been a continual bugbear. On many, many days during a stifling spell of scorching weather, or during the dank, dismal hours of winter, she had longed for fresh country air.

And now she had it.

Olivia tossed the jacket angrily down onto the sofa and walked to her front door. She turned the key and drew back the bolts. It was a dreadful morning but that didn't matter. She was here in the country at least. She should be feeling happy. Paul had done her a favour— he had precipitated the move here; his callous behaviour had allowed her to see that she had never really loved him.

But Jake Savage... Olivia frowned and closed her eyes, inhaling a deep breath, filling her lungs with the sweet, damp air. She could hardly believe all that had taken place between them...

On impulse she stepped under the porch and out into the pouring rain.

It was a mad thing to do, but totally invigorating. Olivia tipped her face to the skies and allowed the rain to saturate her. I'm washing away the grime of the city, she thought. Maybe I can wash away all thoughts of Jake Savage and start again... She tried not to think about how completely he had possessed her, how much her body had ached with wanting him, far into the night after he had gone. *Still* ached... She couldn't stop thinking about him. It was infatuation of the most intense kind. 'Please, don't let it be love,' Olivia whispered as the rain drenched her face, 'don't let it be that.'

'Is this a ritual you hope to perform every morning? If I'd known I'd have made a point of getting here earlier!'

Olivia spun around, her heart beating wildly at the sound of his voice. Jake Savage stood a few feet away, dressed in a long waxed raincoat with two golden Labradors sitting obediently at his feet, watching her make an absolute fool of herself.

'Don't let my presence make any difference,' he drawled, leaning nonchalantly on the gate. 'Go right ahead. I never expected this sort of entertainment so early in the morning. It's quite, quite fascinating.'

Olivia's face flamed with embarrassment; she half expected to see steam coming off her body, so great was the blush that enveloped her. 'What are you doing here?' she asked in a voice that would have frozen water. 'It's rather early in the morning for social calls, isn't it?'

'I'm walking the dogs.' Ebony eyes speared her face. 'Be warned, I do it every morning at around this time. So, if you feel the need to perform this little rite every day and don't wish me to be a witness, I suggest you either set your alarm clock a little earlier or wait until after breakfast.'

Olivia glared at him, hating the cool tone of his voice. 'You think I'm crazy?' she demanded.

He lifted broad shoulders. 'No idea,' he drawled, 'but you're different.' His mouth curled. 'I like it.'

'I don't do this sort of thing usually, you know!' Olivia retorted, angered and embarrassed by his cool demeanour. 'It was just...' She hesitated, trying to come up with a reason for her madness. 'Well, the air smelt so wonderful and the rain's so soft and fresh—'

Dark brows rose in amusement. 'You don't have to justify your actions to me, Olivia. If you want to dance naked on the roof of your house then feel free to go right ahead!' His lips curled provokingly. 'You don't, I suppose?'

She glared. 'No, I do not!'

'Pity.' The ebony eyes focused speculatively. 'It would be a refreshing change.'

'And what happened last night, was that a refreshing change too?' Olivia retorted abruptly. 'Did you have sex with me because you were bored?'

There was a moment of tense silence. The firm mouth tightened ominously. 'No. I had sex because I was attracted to you,' he replied evenly. 'As you were to me.' He gave a brief command to the dogs to stay where they were and then walked towards her. 'It was a compulsion that took us both by surprise. You know that.'

Olivia schooled her expression carefully. 'Do I?'

'Oh, I think so.' He gazed at her narrowly, his expression unreadable. 'Aren't you cold, standing there like that?' he enquired smoothly. 'You look pretty chilled.'

'I'm fine!' Olivia glanced down briefly at her wet gown and matching silk negligée, which clung revealingly to her body. 'But I'll go in anyway—'

His mouth slanted. 'Don't feel you have to rush in on my account,' he murmured. 'I'm enjoying the view.'

He was near her now and Olivia felt the overwhelming strength of his presence. It was like a magnet, drawing her close, holding her steady, making her wait.

She watched as Jake Savage's gaze lingered on her body and felt an automatic stirring deep in her stomach. So long since last night, she thought despairingly, and yet no time at all.

'You like getting wet?' His voice was deep, husky. Olivia swallowed and tried to control the primitive urge that was stirring within her.

'I. . . I told you, it was just a spur-of-the-moment thing. Maybe the country's making me crazy.'

'Good.' The dark eyes gleamed. 'I like crazy people. Especially beautiful ones, with silky buttercup hair and blazing blue eyes.' He raised a hand and lifted a damp tendril from her face.

'Don't!' Olivia jerked her head away and took a pace back. 'You can't do this.'

'Do what?' He looked at Olivia's suddenly rigid face with mild interest. 'What can't I do?'

'You know!' She shivered and wrapped her arms around her body in a defensive gesture. 'I haven't forgotten what you said last night.'

The dark eyes were steady. 'Which was?'

Olivia glared. She felt an overwhelming urge to stamp her feet, but one glance down at her soggy mules told her that that would be rather difficult. She raised her head and focused sharply on the handsome face. 'No ties, no complications, no relationships!' she repeated swiftly. 'You see what a good memory I have?' she added unsteadily.

'Excellent,' Jake agreed. 'Does it extend to remembering the pleasure we discovered too?' Olivia gasped a breath, unable to reply as her mind immediately swung back to the intimacies they had shared. 'Yes, I can see that it does,' he murmured softly, watching her expression. 'That's good.'

Olivia felt a stillness come over her. She focused sapphire eyes on the handsome face. 'Is it?' she whispered.

'You know it is.' He leant forward and kissed her mouth and the familiar desire flared into life. 'An uncomplicated arrangement, Olivia. . .that's what I want. Each of us knowing where we stand from the outset. No ties, no long-term view—'

'Pleasure on demand,' Olivia replied flatly.

'*Mutual* pleasure, yes,' Jake answered. His mouth slid down to cover hers again, lean, strong hands held the slender arch of her neck as his kiss deepened, as his body sought to convince her.

Olivia shivered. He knew the power he had over her and he was using it unmercifully. 'I. . . I don't know. I've never. . . I mean. . .' She swallowed as his lips kissed away the wetness from her throat, struggling to speak, to think coherently. 'Jake!' Her voice was pleading now. 'I'm not used to. . .to this kind of thing.'

The firm mouth hardened perceptibly. 'Do you think I'd be interested if you were?' He drew back, releasing her from his compelling touch. His eyes flashed with intensity. 'I want you.'

'And if I say no?'

'You won't.'

Olivia pursed her lips at the arrogance of the statement. 'But if I do?'

He lifted his broad shoulders in a shrug. It seemed as though the prospect that she might refuse his audacious proposition didn't trouble him at all. 'Then last night will just be a pleasant memory, won't it, Olivia?'

He turned suddenly, called to his dogs, raised his hand in a casual farewell and disappeared in the mist of rain.

# CHAPTER THREE

OLIVIA stood in the rain, staring into space, long after Jake Savage's figure had disappeared, trying to make sense of what he had said, trying to convince herself that she wasn't tempted by such a cool, cynical proposition. Sex. It was just about sex! No mention of feelings, or emotions. . .or love.

Olivia gave a short laugh. Love? What was the point of pretending, of praying that such an emotion would ever come her way? She had foolishly imagined that love had played a part in her relationship with Paul, and look how that had ended up: he had run off and married Ella, her secretary!

Olivia frowned, remembering the humiliation, the sympathetic, pitying faces that had been hers to endure for weeks on end until the sale of the cottage had gone through. She didn't want to have to go through that again. . .never again! She shivered and turned to go inside. Maybe, she thought miserably, cynical Jake Savage had the right idea after all.

By the middle of the morning, Olivia had finished all of her self-appointed tasks. It hadn't been worth doing too much—the decorators were due to arrive in a few days' time—so she had spent much of her time on the phone, finding a firm that would be able to install central heating in double-quick time and another that would deliver a skip to cart away all the rubbish she planned to throw out.

She hunted through her luggage and donned the

leaving present given to her by her firm. Not exactly the two most stylish items she had in her possession, she thought, glancing down at her all-enveloping attire, but definitely the most useful. The raincoat, long and waterproof—not dissimilar to the one Jake had worn earlier—plus matching green wellingtons would be invaluable in the weeks and months and years to come.

She set out briskly, taking the route through the orchard of apple and plum trees, where she planned eventually to install her tea garden, to the gate at the bottom that led directly on to the footpath and then down into the picturesque village below.

Half an hour later and the weather definitely looked as if it was brightening, Olivia tipped back her hood as she entered the little side-street and looked up at the sky. Good. A large patch of blue on the horizon. There would be sun later if they were lucky.

The village looked a picture, with its Victorian-style lampposts, and huge hanging baskets and window-boxes of gorgeous spring flowers seeming to be attached to every cottage.

Olivia strolled around the village. It seemed a friendly place. Most people smiled at her as they passed; a few even bothered to say hello. Such a contrast to the impersonal air of the city, she thought.

She came upon the veterinary surgery almost by accident. She had been concentrating so hard for all of the morning, not allowing herself to think about Jake, and now here she was, standing in front of the shiny brass plaque which bore his name as if it had always been her intended destination.

'If you've come to see how the dog is faring, then I'm afraid you're out of luck.'

Olivia controlled her breathing and swivelled around to find Jake Savage walking towards her.

His mouth curled. 'Don't look so surprised to see me,' he drawled. 'This is my place of work, after all!'

'I wasn't!' Olivia glanced away, disconcerted by his direct gaze. The long coat had been discarded. He was dressed smartly in a tweed jacket and dark trousers and looked every inch the country gentleman. 'Where. . .is he, then?'

'At my place. The surgery's rather full at the moment, and as he's a non-paying guest—'

'If it's a question of money,' Olivia flashed, 'I'll pay for his treatment.'

Jake had climbed the three stone steps that led up to the glossy green door of the surgery. 'It's not.' His voice was curt as he looked down at her. 'Business is booming. Don't worry, I often put the overflow up at my house.'

'How is he?' Olivia asked quietly. 'I. . . I meant to ask you this morning.'

Ebony eyes speared her face. 'And I meant to tell you, but if you remember I was distracted rather badly. There were other, far more pressing subjects on my mind. The dog's fine,' he added swiftly, observing Olivia's flushed expression with an enigmatic expression. 'Nothing to worry about. He found the energy to eat a hearty breakfast this morning and will no doubt be joining my two dogs on our regular morning walks in no time.'

'That's good.'

'Yes, it is.' He waited a moment, watching Olivia's face, and when she made no further effort to speak he opened the door to the surgery. 'Do you want to come inside?'

'No. Jake. . .'

He paused, one hand holding his leather briefcase, the other on the handle of the door, watching her mobile expression with a scrutiny that unnerved her. 'Yes?'

She sensed a sardonic undertone and the thought crossed her mind that he was playing with her. Maybe he didn't want her, maybe it was all just a game. Or maybe, she thought, watching the steely expression, deep down he had known that as soon as he opened the door and made as if to go inside she would call him back.

Am I really being so transparent? she thought, focusing speculatively on the arrogant, assured figure that stood before her. She wished her heart wasn't thudding quite so painfully. No complications, he had said—for him maybe, but for her? She released a steadying breath. The feeling of destiny hadn't diminished, that was the problem. She still felt as if they were meant to be together—one way or another.

'Olivia?' The deep voice was seductive. 'Did you have something you wished to say?'

'I. . . I. . .' She struggled to find her voice. How could she say it? To tell him here, like this, in the middle of the street, that she wanted to continue to be his lover?

'Is it about this morning?' The dark brows were raised questioningly.

But surely she had to grab this opportunity? It would probably mean emotional suicide in the long term. But the alternative? To refuse him? Never to experience his touch again? That was unthinkable.

An elderly man passed by, pausing momentarily to acknowledge Jake. Two other women crossed the street towards the surgery, casting Olivia a curious glance as they came near. She couldn't do it. Not now, anyway, not in the middle of the village. Did he really expect her to?

'I. . . I just wondered why there are so many floral decorations around?' It was the only thing she could think of to say. She swallowed, feeling like a schoolgirl with a crush on a teacher.

Jake frowned, glancing across at the huge baskets of spring bulbs that were hanging from every available position. 'It's traditional at this time of year. A way of celebrating.'

'Celebrating what?'

He took his time answering and Olivia could see from his expression that Jake was making an effort to focus his thoughts. 'The beginning of May. We have a May ball,' he added abruptly, 'for the villagers.'

'Tonight?' There was a slight nod and Olivia smiled, her eyes glued to the stunning features. 'It sounds like fun,' she replied with forced gaiety.

'You think so?' Jake shrugged, boredom creeping into his expression. 'Maybe you'll enjoy it, then—I'm not particularly enamoured with the occasion.'

Olivia tried to keep the disappointment from her voice. 'You. . .won't be attending?'

'Unfortunately, yes.' He looked at her and a grim curve twisted his mouth. 'It comes with the territory.'

Olivia frowned. 'I don't understand,' she murmured. 'What territory?'

Jet eyes probed hers. 'Come on! Are you trying to tell me you really don't know?'

'Know what?'

He turned towards her, closing the door behind him as he descended the steps. 'Look around you, Olivia,' he drawled. 'Go on, do it!' he commanded roughly, turning her bodily to face the cobbled side-street, uncaring of the looks of the passers-by. 'Note every house, every brick, every inch of real estate. See the high street beyond? The village green beyond that? The pub and the church and the duck pond?'

Olivia swung away from his hold, slanting him a puzzled glance. 'I see it.' She shrugged, sensing the unexplained intensity. 'So what?'

'It's mine,' he announced evenly; 'every last brick, every last blade of grass.' There was a pause as he looked around. 'All mine.'

Olivia frowned, not sure how to react. He looked serious enough, but surely what he said couldn't be true; people didn't own whole villages any more—did they? She shook her head. 'You're. . .joking, surely?'

'Do I look as if I'm joking?' The smouldering eyes were fixed on her face.

'But I. . .I thought you were a vet!' Olivia replied, still struggling to assimilate this outrageous piece of information.

'I am. It's not beyond the realms of possibility that veterinary surgeons can be landowners too, you know.'

She looked around her in wonderment. 'You actually own the whole of this village?'

'I can see you're impressed,' he replied drily.

'Well, of course I'm impressed!' she answered lightly. 'What did you expect?' She spun around, looking at the pretty houses, unaware of Jake Savage's brooding gaze. 'It's so lovely! Why didn't you mention it before?'

'When would you have suggested—before or after we made love?'

Olivia glared at him. 'That's not a particularly nice thing to say!'

'Maybe I'm not a particularly nice person!' His

expression had altered dangerously. She could feel the latent power, the anger seething below the surface. 'You would have said yes to my proposition immediately this morning if you'd have known I was a man of substantial means, then?'

There was silence. Olivia's gaze rested on the hard, unsmiling mouth. The word 'destiny' rose like a spectre before her very eyes to haunt her. How could she say yes to him now? How *could* she? With Jake Savage looking at her like this? With him thinking such awful things? 'That's a. . .a despicable thing to say!' Her voice shook with anger. 'You think I care about. . .about your *wealth*! How dare you?'

'It may be despicable.' Dark eyes glinted steel. 'But that doesn't stop it being true, does it? In my experience women can so easily be seduced by power and influence, not to mention wealth—'

'*Some* women!' Olivia cut in. 'Not all!'

'And I do remember you telling me how much importance you placed on money when we first met,' Jake continued evenly. 'Do you remember?'

'I didn't mean it the way you think!' Olivia replied, outraged. 'It doesn't matter that much. I just meant it can make life a lot easier, that's all!'

'So my owning all this,' he gestured expansively with his arm, 'means my life must be a bowl of cherries, then, does it?' The attractive mouth hardened perceptively. 'Don't look so worried! It doesn't have to alter the way things stand between us, Olivia. Neither of us is interested in a messy, emotional entanglement. You've had your fingers burnt recently and so have I.'

'You?' Olivia shook her head. 'I can't believe you allowed any woman to get near enough!'

'Believe it.' His reply was curt. 'The slip-up occurred

when I was at a low ebb, not thinking particularly straight.' Jake's eyes darkened as they came to rest on Olivia's face. 'Don't worry,' he drawled, 'I won't allow it to happen again.'

Olivia's gaze narrowed bitterly. 'Of course I understand things a lot more clearly now!' she flared. 'It's the classic lord-of-the-manor syndrome: you see, you want, you have—or at least you try to have! Isn't that how it used to be in the olden days? Rather an outdated concept, I would have thought, for a man of the nineties...'

She had hit a sore spot, Olivia saw that immediately, but Jake covered up his annoyance swiftly. 'You are, of course, referring to my invitation this morning,' he drawled. A dark brow rose quizzically. 'Tell me, why has it disturbed you so? I would have thought a woman with your sophisticated background would be well used to the ways of the world, well used to the ways of lecherous men like myself.'

'I never said you were lecherous!'

The attractive mouth curled. 'No? Well, that's something, I suppose.'

'You could be, though!' Olivia added impulsively. 'It wouldn't surprise me to find that this morning's experience is standard treatment for anyone under thirty wearing a skirt!'

He smiled. Damn him, he smiled! 'You're deliberately trying to make me angry,' he murmured. 'I wonder why?'

'Maybe because I don't like you!' Olivia retorted. 'I'm angry because you infuriate me.'

'You're angry because I excite you and I've dared to do something about it!' Jake replied tersely. 'Stop kidding yourself and face up to reality! We've made love and, no matter how hard you try to deny it, you can't wait for it to happen again!'

The unsayable thing had been said. The tension peaked. Olivia felt it like a tangible thing, hanging in the air between them. She clenched her hands into balls at her sides and forced herself to breathe evenly, to think rationally. There could be no scene here. No screaming match. He didn't understand and she couldn't explain. How could she explain to a man who was so hard and cynical and *unhappy* all that she had felt and dreamed in that first moment of seeing him?

'You really don't like me very much, do you?' she whispered.

'Like you?' There was a painful pause as he considered. He *wants* to hurt me, Olivia thought miserably. He really doesn't care at all. Dark brows were raised reflectively. 'To tell you the truth, I haven't given it much thought. I desire you,' he added fluidly, 'I want us to be lovers, but that's a totally different thing.'

'Yes, it is.' Olivia gulped a breath. 'I think I'd better be going,' she murmured as the surgery door opened and a young girl carrying a pet hamster in a cage emerged. 'Tell me,' she asked, turning back suddenly, 'do you always get what you want?'

There was a moment of hesitation and then the hard mouth curved without humour. 'What do you think?'

'Then why aren't you happy?' Olivia enquired bitingly. 'Why do I get the impression that you hate yourself as well as everything around you?'

'I have my reasons.' He was *admitting* it? Olivia scanned the handsome face and tried to read something into the enigmatic expression. 'But they're personal.' The harsh mouth curved. 'Funnily enough, Olivia, I'm not in the habit of divulging my innermost thoughts whilst standing in the middle of the street.'

'Do you *ever*?'

Her voice was quiet. Jake threw her a vexed look and then turned away. 'I've got work to do.'

'Will. . .will I see you later?' The sentence was dragged out of her. Do I have no pride? Olivia wondered.

He stared at her unintelligibly, as if his thoughts were somewhere else, far away. 'Maybe.'

'At the May ball?'

He shrugged. 'I've told you, I'll be there.'

'Where will you be?'

The voice made them both turn. Olivia's startled gaze came to rest on a pretty, dark-haired young woman who kissed Jake on the cheek and immediately linked her arm through his in a proprietorial manner. 'Introducing yourself to our new resident, Jake?' Her voice sounded cheerful enough, but the eyes told a different story; hard and green and quite ominously intent.

'We were just discussing the May ball,' Jake replied. 'Olivia asked about the flowers.'

'Oh, Olivia, is it?' The green eyes flashed venom for an instant. 'Well, that's the intimacy of village life for you! Barely twenty-four hours a resident and it's first-name terms already!' There was a slight pause. Olivia felt the tension, although she didn't understand its cause. 'Come, now! Aren't you going to introduce us, Jake?' the hard voice continued smoothly. 'I'm sure Olivia will be only too glad to make some more acquaintances.'

'Sophie, this is Olivia Hamilton. Olivia, this is Sophie Carlton.'

The introduction was terse and without preamble. Olivia held out her hand, forcing her mouth into a friendly smile, even though she was aware that it wouldn't be welcome. 'Nice to meet you.'

'I'm a friend of Jake's—a good friend.' Sophie ignored Olivia's traditional greeting. 'You've moved into Honeysuckle Cottage, haven't you?'

'Er. . .yes, that's right.' Olivia replied, lowering her hand to thrust it into the pocket of her coat. 'It's a lovely little place.'

'So how it is you two are already acquainted?'

'Umm. . .'Olivia cast a quick glance at Jake, who stared back with an implacable expression. 'I had a bit of trouble with my taxi and Jake was passing. . .'

'Olivia's taxi driver drove like a maniac,' Jake added smoothly. 'He collided with the Range Rover.'

'And you gave Olivia a lift to her cottage, I suppose.' Sophie didn't look best pleased. 'Come, now, admit it!' she accused lightly, glancing up into Jake's handsome face. 'You engineered the whole thing just so you could have your wicked way with her!'

Olivia felt herself grow warm. It was a joke, wasn't it? Those hard, attractive green eyes didn't actually *know*, did they?

Jake's mouth widened into a predatory smile. He looked suddenly dangerous and Olivia felt herself grow faint with anxiety as he spoke. 'Oh, I've already had my wicked way, Sophie,' he drawled. 'You know me, always quick to spot a pretty face and a good pair of legs! No female's safe in the village whilst I'm around!' He bent down and kissed Sophie briefly on the cheek, before extricating himself smoothly from the young woman's grip. 'Now, if you'll excuse me, ladies.' He glanced briefly in Olivia's direction. 'I have work to do!'

'I do hope you're not going to make a fool of yourself over him,' Sophie announced once Jake had safely entered the surgery.

Olivia frowned, startled by the young woman's directness. 'I beg your pardon?'

'Snaring Jake Savage!' The attractive mouth curved knowingly. 'Oh, come on! Don't bother trying to look innocent! That's what's on your mind, isn't it?'

Olivia focused her gaze on the carefully made-up face. 'I don't *snare* men!' she retorted crisply.

'Maybe not ordinarily, but then Jake Savage is no ordinary man. He's. . .he's special. I've known him for years. Of all the people in the whole of this village, I probably know him the best.' The green eyes glinted fire suddenly. 'He's mine!' Sophie hissed. 'Always has been, always will be! So keep your hands off! Jake needs me, just like I need him. We've been through too much together for him to even look at anyone else.' She lifted her slim shoulders. 'Oh, I know he has a fling from time to time; what man doesn't? And women, *all* women, find him irresistible,' she added. 'But that doesn't matter. That's not important. He knows I understand about that. He knows I'm waiting for him. When he decides to settle down I'll be here. *I'll* be the one he wants.' She narrowed her gaze and stung Olivia with a look. 'He's made that clear enough to me. Is it clear enough for you, Miss Hamilton? Have you got the picture?'

It was a disturbing speech, not least because of the absolute authority and the desperate air of intensity with which it was delivered. Olivia hesitated slightly. The green eyes were still fixed upon her face and she

wondered for a fleeting moment if the pretty young
woman was slightly deranged. 'I think so,' she managed
to murmur at last. 'Now if. . .if you'll excuse me,' she
added swiftly. 'I've got some shopping to do.'

Olivia moved past the short, slender figure and
walked briefly towards the main street without looking
back, even though she knew Sophie's glittering gaze
was fixed upon her.

# CHAPTER FOUR

OLIVIA's hands were shaking. She thrust them under the black velvet wrap she was wearing and looked up at the lights that shone from every one of the thirty or so windows of the impressive Georgian mansion house.

The village taxi service was working overtime. No sooner had it dropped off Olivia than it returned with another party, and then another and another. It seemed as if every one of the village's inhabitants had put on their finery and come to the May ball.

The music was vaguely classical, as befitted the occasion. Olivia handed her wrap to an attendant in the hall and accepted her ticket with a nervous smile.

Entering Jake Savage's domain was awe-inspiring to say the least. She had expected grandeur, but not on such a huge scale. If the hallway was impressive, with its sweeping carved staircase, fine paintings and sculptures, then the ballroom, with its gilt and ornaments, was magnificent; large tapestries decorated one wall, ornate mirrors another, paintings everywhere she looked.

There was a string quartet situated at one end of the long room, and Olivia found her gaze drawn towards it. The music was beautiful, like something out of a fairy tale. Several couples were already gliding around the room.

Olivia stepped forward over the threshold of the ballroom. She wanted to be here and yet common sense told her she shouldn't have come.

Instinctively she smoothed nervous hands over the folds of her skirt. She had chosen to wear a full-length silk dress in lilac for the occasion; a simple scoop neck, and sleek-fitting skirt and bodice. No frills, no unnecessary adornments, just perfectly cut fabric that skimmed her figure in all the right places and revealed the smoothness of her skin at her throat and shoulders.

Olivia managed a smile at one or two familiar faces, met whilst out shopping that morning, and took a few more paces forward, willing her nerves to disappear.

Where was Jake? That was her only thought, the only reason for coming. How long did she have to wait like this?

And then she saw him.

There was no one else but him. Everything, every one of the hundred or so villagers faded into insignificance.

He looked magnificent, dressed in immaculate evening attire; deepest jet against crisp white, every line emphasising the powerful frame, the compelling physique.

Slowly she turned, savouring the moment, aware of the increase in her heartbeat as her eyes rested on the handsome face.

He walked towards her; slow, measured steps down the length of the ballroom. Stunning, magnetic eyes never leaving her face.

Her dress rustled deliciously as she moved across the wood-blocked floor to meet him. She felt like a princess in a fairy tale, like Cinderella coming to the ball, waiting for her prince. . .

'My dance, I think?' His voice was deep and immensely seductive. Olivia felt the animal vibrancy as he came near. Her pulses were thudding violently and it took all of her control to appear reasonably composed. A dark brow quirked when she didn't immediately reply. 'You can waltz, I take it?'

Olivia let out a tense breath. 'After a fashion,' she murmured.

The seductive mouth curled slightly. 'Well, I promise to do my best not to stand on your toes,' he drawled. 'Now shall we begin and get this charade over with?'

'Charade?' Olivia looked up into his face. 'What do you mean?'

His mouth twisted coolly. 'Well, you don't actually *want* to dance with me, do you, Olivia?'

He gave her no time to reply. Taking her into his arms, he swept her around the room, guiding her gracefully in time to the music. It *was* like something out of a fairy tale and, despite Olivia's determination to stay aloof and unmoved, the perfect nature of the occasion and the pleasure of being physically close again to Jake overrode all other considerations.

As her confidence improved Olivia found herself sinking into Jake's arms, relaxing quite intimately against the taut, hard frame.

'That was quite an entrance you made just now,' he drawled huskily as they negotiated their second loop around the ballroom. 'I hardly recognised you. You've put your hair up; it looks good like that.'

'I... I thought I'd better make an effort,' Olivia murmured breathlessly, conscious of every inch of his body, of the way it felt to be so close to him. She wondered how long the sleek chignon would last. It emphasised the graceful lines of her neck, and revealed the elegance of her antique onyx earrings, but it had been the devil to get right. 'The lady in the village store impressed upon me the importance of the occasion,' she added lightly. She glanced around her as she danced. 'It's all very grand.'

'You didn't imagine the village capable of such sophistication, I suppose?' Jake enquired drily.

'Not exactly, I have to admit that such grandeur as this has come as a bit of a shock.' Olivia glanced up swiftly, contemplating the chiselled features, trying to gauge the mood that lay beneath the mask. 'Am I allowed to tell you that I think you have a gorgeous house?' she murmured as the rich palette of colours from the tapestries flew by for the second time. 'I really hadn't expected such elegance and beauty.'

'Neither had I.' Jake smiled, his lips curling seductively as Olivia blushed a delicate shade of pink. He gazed down at her in amusement. 'Embarrassment, Olivia? A woman of the world and you're not used to compliments?'

'Not from you, no!' Olivia tilted her head backwards to get away from his gaze, her eyes alighting on the fine mouldings and impressive chandelier that decorated the ceiling above.

'I'm sorry. . .about the way I spoke to you this morning.' He didn't sound particularly sorry, but something told Olivia that that had more to do with the rarity of such a statement than the fact that he didn't mean it. 'You caught me at a bad moment.'

Her heart thudded violently. 'You mean. . .when I saw you in the village?' she murmured swiftly. 'Then?'

'When else?'

Olivia hesitated, keeping her face averted from his, conscious of the sick feeling deep in her stomach. 'I thought. . .maybe. . .' Her voice trailed away.

'You thought perhaps I meant much earlier this

morning,' he finished for her. 'Like at seven a.m., with the rain pouring down from the heavens?'

Olivia glanced into his face and blushed. 'I just wondered.'

'Well, wonder no more.' His voice was deep and sexy, incredibly sexy. 'What I said I meant. I still want you.'

She drew back from him a fraction, biting her bottom lip self-consciously, disturbed and overwhelmed by the intensity of his words.

'You know, when you do that you remind me of somebody,' Jake murmured quietly.

'I do?' Olivia looked into his face, narrowing her eyes in query, using the moment to reassert her composure. 'Who?'

The directness of her question seemed to trigger something in him. The reflective, relaxed expression disappeared, to be replaced by a mask of icy control that shuttered his expression completely. 'Forget it. It doesn't matter.'

'I'd like to know,' Olivia murmured. 'Can't you tell me?'

'I said it doesn't matter!' The deep voice was abrupt. 'I don't know why I even mentioned it.'

Olivia glanced away and concentrated on holding herself aloof again. She hated the way he could devastate her with just a few sharp words.

The music was coming to an end. When it stopped she tried to pull apart from Jake but he held her firm, one large hand pressing against the base of her spine, the other still clasping her fingers.

'My mother,' he murmured, looking long and hard into the clear blue of her eyes. 'You remind me of my mother.' Olivia watched silently as the attractive mouth curled a little. 'Satisfied?'

She felt moved and she wasn't quite sure why. There was an intolerable ache inside. So close to this man, and yet so far from understanding any part of him, she thought.

'Is she here?' Olivia made her voice sound light, conscious that she was treading on eggshells.

'No.' The reply was terse. Dark, dangerous eyes probed hers for a moment and then he tugged her across the dance floor. 'Come on,' he announced suddenly. 'I think we both deserve a drink.'

Waiters mingled with glasses and delicious-looking canapés on trays. As Jake got caught up in conversation with a group of villagers Olivia took her champagne and wandered over to examine some of the paintings in more detail. The strength of his presence was pure torture. She had come here this evening vowing all sorts of things, making herself all sorts of promises, which had been broken the minute she had set eyes on Jake Savage. She desperately needed a moment away from him to sort her feelings out.

'I suppose you think you've got something special!' The sharp voice made Olivia jump slightly, but she kept her eyes glued to the canvas in front of her, feigning an interest in the Victorian family group.

Olivia's peripheral vision told her Sophie was wearing red. She could smell the cloying scent of her perfume mixed with alcohol, feel the venom in her glare, even without seeing it. 'Why should I?' Olivia kept her voice light, feeling the tension and unhappiness beside her like a living, tangible thing.

'I saw the looks you were giving him!' Sophie continued. 'Don't start thinking one dance means something! See the May queen over there?' She pointed to a young girl dressed in white with a circle of spring flowers in her hair. 'Jake was dancing with her before you made your entrance—very close they were getting, too. The best you can hope for is to add your name to a very long list of sexual conquests!'

Olivia glanced sideways at last. 'And you?' she queried, keeping her expression calm, refusing to dwell on the deliberate words of torment. 'Are you on that list?'

She saw the girl pale slightly, but Sophie recovered quickly. '*I'm* not a tramp!' She looked Olivia up and down pointedly. 'Jake respects me. I told you we. . .we have an understanding.'

Olivia looked back at the picture and tried to keep her countenance calm. She wanted to defuse the situation, but she didn't know how. 'So you mentioned earlier today. The children look sweet, don't they?' she murmured, gesturing towards the blonde ringlets and pretty dresses of the classical Victorian family pose in front of her. 'I wonder what it was like to live then?'

'Essentially much the same as now, I should imagine.' Jake's deep voice sounded slightly bitter behind Olivia's right shoulder. 'Love, hate, misery—those emotions don't alter, do they?'

'No. . .no, I suppose not.' Olivia inhaled a steadying breath and took a sip of champagne. She glanced across towards Sophie as she drank and saw the young woman's expression alter. Jake must know how she feels, Olivia thought miserably. No man could misinterpret those looks, surely?

'Are. . .are they relatives of yours?' Olivia continued, turning to look enquiringly into Jake's face.

'Yes.' His gaze. God! There should be a danger sign

linked to such a look, Olivia thought. Unashamedly sensual, vitally intense...hooded dark eyes that told the world how much he wanted to make love to her. Olivia blushed scarlet, conscious of Sophie close at her shoulder. Was *she* aware of that look? Had she guessed that they had already made love?

'Er... Sophie and I have just been talking about dancing,' Olivia murmured desperately. 'The ball is part of the May queen's official duties, I understand.'

'It is.' Jake turned and smiled warmly into Sophie's pretty face. 'Did Sophie tell you what a beautiful May queen she made last year? The whole village commented on how good she was and how wonderful she looked.'

Olivia worked hard at hiding her surprise. 'Er... no...no, she didn't.'

'I had always wanted to be queen ever since I was a little girl,' Sophie murmured quietly. Her expression changed dramatically and suddenly she looked lost and lonely, not like the hard-faced young woman of a moment ago. 'It was just a shame... I mean, I wish that...that things had been different. If Edward had been—'

'Come on. Let's dance!' Jake took hold of Sophie's hand, shooting Olivia a glance she didn't understand, and pulled the former May queen over to the middle of the dance floor.

Olivia watched the couple together. They looked good. If she was being absolutely honest she'd admit Sophie and Jake looked perfect together; both dark, both good-looking. There was a familiarity between them that Olivia envied; he was holding her close, smiling encouragingly as he looked down into the pretty face, listening as she spoke.

Jake spent a great deal of the evening with Sophie. She clung onto his arm as he mingled with the guests, laughing and chattering, playing the part of lady of the manor and doing so very effectively. Olivia hated the jealousy she felt. She didn't want to be affected by such strength of feeling—it was anathema to her, an alien emotion. She wished she could just walk away and forget she had ever allowed Jake Savage to make love to her.

'Do you want to come and see the invalid?'

Olivia spun around. She had been standing in front of a tapestry, trying to pluck up the courage to leave, staring with unseeing eyes so that the colours and design merged into one.

So much smiling, when inside she felt as miserable as hell.

She raised fine, arched brows and played it cool as she looked up into his face. 'I beg your pardon?'

Jake was alone. His mouth curved knowingly, as if he was aware of the game she was playing. 'The dog. Would you like to see how he is?'

She allowed herself time to consider, knowing all the while exactly what her answer would be. 'If it's not too much trouble,' she murmured after a suitable pause. Her voice sounded good; casual, indifferent. 'Where is he exactly?'

'Causing havoc in the kitchens, driving my house-keeper wild.' Jake removed her empty glass from her fingers and placed it on a passing tray. 'Follow me.'

She hesitated, wary now of being alone with him. 'But you have your guests to consider,' she murmured glancing around. 'I wouldn't want you to neglect your duties—'

'Frightened of being alone with me?' he drawled.

There was a twist of the attractive mouth. 'Don't worry, Olivia. I won't lock you up and keep you captive. We have no dungeons here.' He moved closer. She felt the animal vibrancy, the danger of the predator, camouflaged beneath the evening suit, as he reached out to her. 'I too believe in freedom of movement, freedom of speech.' He paused, tugging her towards him, making a mockery of their first conversation. 'Freedom of choice.'

'Jake! People are looking at us.'

An ebony brow was raised. 'So?'

'Don't you care?'

'About what?' The attractive mouth twisted. 'I'm only taking you to see a patient. Unless you had other ideas?'

Olivia tilted her chin. 'Of course I didn't!' she flashed, assuring herself that he couldn't read her mind. 'I'll see the dog later,' she delivered evenly, praying for help with her defiance. 'After all, the party's in full swing and—'

'Now!' His gaze told her he was in charge. He took her hand in a firm and uncompromising grasp. 'The offer's open for a limited period only.'

'But... Jake!' He wasn't listening. He didn't care about the interest he was arousing, about the fact that Olivia could hardly keep up with his determined stride as he led her across the well-polished floor towards a door at the far end of the room.

The gathering parted, like the sea for Moses, Olivia thought despairingly, trying not to notice the interest on most people's faces, conscious of a flash of familiar red taffeta as Jake continued to tug her forward.

'Would you mind slowing down?' Olivia gasped once they were through a side-door and out of sight of the partygoers. 'Neither these shoes nor this dress were meant for running in!'

'I wasn't aware I was going particularly fast,' Jake drawled.

'Well, you were!' Olivia glanced around at the panelled corridor and released a tense breath. 'Is this the way to the kitchen?'

She saw the look of amusement flicker across the rugged face. 'Where else? Or do you imagine that I'm about to lead you to an anonymous room with a four-poster bed in it?' He paused and then in the next moment he had pulled her towards him and she was suddenly, shockingly in the curve of his arms, feeling the strength of him pressing against her slim body. 'Do you *want* me to lead you to somewhere like that?'

'Please don't!' Olivia shook her head, her forget-me-not eyes wide with uncertainty. 'Don't tease!'

'Who said anything about teasing?' His voice was deep, mesmeric. 'It's a genuine question.'

She swallowed. 'Look, Jake... I... I don't know if I can handle this. I don't understand you... or... or understand the way I feel, or—'

'Don't make it complicated.' His voice was husky and very, very soft. He lifted a finger and brushed her lips, then moved away a strand of hair from her face. 'Think simple. Think of what you want. Life's better that way. You told me so yourself.'

Olivia frowned, her breathing coming in short, rapid bursts. There was a constant, erotic ache in her pelvis, an awareness surging through her body that stopped just short of her head, numbing her brain's powers of sensibility. 'Did I?' she queried weakly.

'You did.' He dropped a kiss onto her mouth. 'Don't you remember?'

She considered his smouldering gaze. 'I'm. . . I'm not a tramp,' she murmured, thinking of Sophie's words.

'If you were I wouldn't want you.'

'But you do?' Her voice was barely audible.

His mouth curled. 'Haven't I made that clear enough by now? I don't waste effort on saying things that aren't true—' There was a flicker of hesitation, a sharp, anguished look that was visible for a fraction of a second, illuminating the depths of Jake Savage's soul. 'At least, not any more.' Olivia heard the edge of steel hiding a multitude of complex emotions in his voice and then it was extinguished suddenly.

'You used to?' It was a whisper of a question. Cautious, almost frightened of itself. Ventured because of an overwhelming need to know, to understand something about this man.

He looked at her. A cold, hard stare that made her tremble deep down inside. Remembering. 'Yes.'

There was a tense pause. Along the darkened corridor and through the oak-panelled door Olivia could hear the band playing and the laughter and the talk of the villagers.

'For more time than I care to remember it became an absolute way of life.'

Olivia shook her head, her expression showing confusion. 'What do you mean?'

'Don't ask.' His voice was flat and hard. He released a short breath and set her free from the circle of his arms. 'I won't tell you, so there's no point. Now come.' He turned away. 'It's time to see the animal.'

He didn't attempt to touch her again. When they finally arrived at the kitchen a glossy black pup with a bandage on his paw scrambled from his basket by the stove and squealed with happiness at the sight of them both.

'Oh, he's a darling!' Olivia knelt down and stroked the silky fur. 'Doesn't he look well? You've worked wonders with him.'

'Amazing what a bath and some food can do, isn't it? Careful of your dress.' Jake bent forward and scooped the animal out of Olivia's arms. 'He'll ruin it. You don't want to have to go back into the ballroom with tufts of fur all over that expensive outfit, do you?'

Olivia rose to her feet and watched as Jake put the animal back into his basket with a firm word of command. There was something wrong and she didn't know what it was. She glanced across at him but there were no clues in his expression—when were there ever?

'What are you going to do with him, once he's fully recovered?' she asked, trying to infuse normality into her voice.

He sat down on the edge of a large wooden table and lifted broad shoulders in an uncaring shrug, loosening the black bow tie at his throat. 'I haven't given it any great thought. No one's come forward to claim him.'

'Can I have him?'

'You?' He seemed a little surprised. 'For good?'

Olivia nodded. 'Yes. He will be company for me.'

He shrugged again. 'Fine. A couple of days, then you can take him.'

'I'll call him Mutt.'

An eyebrow quirked derisively. 'Original.'

Her voice was cool. 'I like it.'

They were antagonists all of a sudden and she didn't know why. He may want me, Olivia thought suddenly, but it's true, he doesn't particularly like me.

'I'm going back to the ballroom.'

'Fine.'

'Aren't you coming?' Olivia asked quietly.

He seemed to drag himself away from somewhere else, from some*one* else maybe. 'Not just yet.'

'Jake. . .' Olivia hesitated. The need to make contact with him was overwhelming suddenly. Not just physically—although God knew the need to touch him again was strong enough—but emotionally. She wanted to know him, she wanted to understand him. 'Is. . .is there something wrong?'

The dark head lifted. It was clear he hadn't heard. 'What?'

'I just wondered. . .' Olivia paused. 'You seem. . . preoccupied.'

Jake released a short laugh that held precious little hint of amusement. 'That's one way of describing it!' He looked across at her. 'So, I'm preoccupied, am I?'

'You seem that way.' Olivia shook her head, glancing back down to stare at Mutt.

'I've had a lot on my mind for some time now,' Jake murmured, 'and, no matter which way I look at it, things don't seem to be getting any better.'

'Can. . .can I help?'

His mouth twisted and he shook his head. 'No.' Silence. Olivia tried not to allow the rejection to hurt her. She glanced down at Mutt again and willed herself to be strong. 'Thanks anyway,' Jake continued in obviously patient tones. 'I'll work it out one way or another. I guess I've had too much to drink; I must be getting maudlin, burdening you with my problems. It doesn't matter.'

'It looks as if it matters,' Olivia murmured, taking a step towards him. 'Whatever it is, it looks as if it matters very much.' She reached out a hand suddenly and touched the angular cheek bone. The gesture seemed to take Jake by surprise. She felt him stiffen slightly and then he relaxed, not moving, not saying anything, transfixed, it seemed, by the softness of her fingers on his skin. Touching him felt good. After a moment Olivia leant forward and brushed her lips across the finely moulded mouth. 'Can't we talk, Jake?' she whispered. 'I'm sure if—'

'No.' His voice was so harsh that it made her jump back as if he had reached out and physically hit her. He closed his eyes briefly, as if rejecting her advances gave him pain, and when he opened them and spoke again his voice was less hurtful than before. 'Go back to the ballroom, Olivia,' he ordered, rising from the table and moving away from her. 'Please, just do as I say and go!'

'Why do you have to be like this?' Olivia demanded suddenly. 'Why can't you tell me anything?'

'Because my problems are no concern of yours, that's why,' Jake answered sharply.

'I had a very interesting conversation with Sophie this morning,' Olivia delivered in ragged tones. 'Actually, she did most of the talking; I just listened.'

Jake's dark eyes narrowed. 'What did she say?'

He looked concerned, as well he might, Olivia thought angrily. 'She's quite devoted to you, isn't she?' Olivia said, working hard at keeping a thread of coolness in her voice. 'A devotion bordering on the obsession, I'd say—'

'We've known each other a long time,' Jake replied crisply. 'Don't waste your time trying to understand!'

It was a hurtful response and Olivia fell silent. She stared at the hard, rigid lines of Jake's face for a moment and then she spun away and left the kitchen without another word.

The May ball was still going strong. Olivia slipped in through the side-door, accepted a canapé and some sparkling mineral water from a passing waiter and was immediately accosted by Sophie once more. It was the last thing she needed.

'Look, I'm not interested in having an argument,' Olivia announced before the scarlet mouth had a chance to say anything. 'So will you just leave me alone?'

'You really do think you're so superior, don't you?' Sophie cried. 'Why can't you just get right away from here?'

Olivia's heart sank. Sophie sounded more than a little drunk.

Jake appeared. Out of the corner of her eye Olivia saw his purposeful stride moving across the ballroom. Sophie saw him too.

'Can't you see you're upsetting him?' she slurred. 'He doesn't need someone like you,' she added, struggling to keep vertical. 'Jake!' she called shrilly. 'Jake, I'm over here!'

Dark eyes glanced in her direction. Olivia saw the gaze and tried to move away, but found herself restrained by Sophie's determined hand on her arm. She glanced down at the scarlet talons and then up into the pale face and matching blood-red lips. 'Would you mind letting go of me?'

'Jake's coming over.'

'I can see that,' Olivia replied stiffly, 'but would you let go of my arm?'

'Sophie, why don't you do as Olivia asks?'

He had joined them both, just as Olivia was beginning to feel genuinely uncomfortable, almost afraid of the woman standing beside her. She released a breath and met his dark gaze, glad of the reassuring strength of his presence.

'Oh, *Olivia* again, is it?'

'Sophie, this is not the time or the place.' Jake put an arm around the slender waist. 'Now, why don't you come along with me? You know you're looking a little tired—'

'Don't treat me like a child!' She pulled away so violently from his embrace that she nearly teetered over on her high heels. 'What do you take me for—a fool?'

'You don't want a scene.' The deep, smooth voice held an edge of warning. 'Whatever you've got to say can be said to me, in private.'

'I don't see why! You've been pretty public yourself today—in the village this morning, remember? You and her looking all intense together!' She flung a wild-eyed look in Olivia's bemused direction. 'It didn't take you long, did it? Our glamorous new resident! Don't you think I can see, that the whole village can see, what's going on between the two of you?'

'You've had too much to drink again,' Jake muttered wearily. 'For heaven's sake, listen to yourself.'

'I don't want to! Do you think I even care?' There were tears now, streaming down the angular face. 'Can't you understand how I *feel*?'

Olivia swallowed back a lump in her own throat. She didn't completely understand any of this, but she recognised misery and anguish when she saw it. The whole village did too. Conversations had stopped, the music had ceased, and an air of embarrassed horror lay like a shroud over the whole proceedings as Jake was

subjected to a shrill volley of unintelligible verbal
abuse.

Olivia stared wide-eyed, watching with a sickening
feeling in her stomach, mesmerised like the rest of the
gathering, by the scene that was so out of place, so
shocking. He stood impassively throughout, cool and
infinitely hard, gazing at Sophie, listening almost as if
what she had to say needed his attention.

Why didn't he do something?

Sophie's agitation was fast turning into hysteria. The
uncomfortable feeling in the hall was growing. Olivia
turned, sickened by the scene, and began threading her
way through the crowds, anxious to get away, to feel
the relief of the cool night air on her face.

And then, just as she reached the door, there was a
sharp sound of hand on face, followed by complete and
utter silence. Olivia glanced back, saw the distraught
scarlet figure in Jake's arms and knew that he had
taken control at last.


'I thought you'd left.'

Olivia watched as Jake leaned against the stone
balustrade. He looked out across the acres of moonlit
parkland that stretched far into the distance and sur-
rounded his impressive home. 'I should have done.'

'It's still early.'

She took a steadying breath. 'I think it would be best
if I went, don't you?'

'Because of the scene in the ballroom?' The
shadowed face turned to observe her.

Olivia hugged her velvet wrap close around her body
and continued to study the moonlit pastures. 'Partly
that, yes.'

'I'm sorry you had to be involved. It was. . . unfortunate.'

Olivia released a disbelieving breath. '*Unfortunate*? Is that all you can say? It was dreadful! She was so. . . so desperate!'

'It's been building up for months. Sophie's having a hard time of it at the moment. She's not a well woman.'

'I could see that for myself,' Olivia replied swiftly. 'Where is she now?'

'Home.' Jake sounded weary. 'I took her there myself.'

'You haven't left her on her own, surely?' Olivia queried. 'She was in no fit state—'

'Will you let up?' The edge of steel in his voice indicated that patience was wearing thin. 'I'm not that stupid. There's no need to worry yourself. Sophie Carlton has a faithful housekeeper to take care of her.'

'She's rich, then, like yourself?'

Jake nodded. 'Oh, yes,' he murmured grimly. 'Quite rich.'

'Not to mention very unhappy,' Olivia added.

'That too,' Jake agreed flatly. 'I suppose you think we're two of a kind.'

Olivia hesitated. The stars were bright in the night sky. She tilted her head and looked for the Great Bear formation—the only one she knew. 'Because of you?' she murmured quietly, her eyes intent on the heavens. 'Is she unhappy because of something you've done?'

'You could say that.' Jake shook his head, running weary fingers through his glossy black hair. He leaned forward, brushing Olivia's velvet wrap with the sleeve of his jacket, resting strong hands on the stone balustrade in front of him, and looked out far into the distance. 'I knew how she felt, of course, but tonight's the first time she's shown her feelings so openly.'

'She hates me,' Olivia murmured.

'No, she doesn't.'

Olivia released an exasperated breath. 'Hell, Jake! Where's your intelligence? Of course she does! It's you too. It's your behaviour that's hurting her—'

'Just drop it!' His voice was rough-edged. 'You don't understand.'

'Doesn't she need a doctor or something?' Olivia asked quietly. 'She seemed pretty. . .' she hesitated, searching for a description that was tactful '. . .intense.'

'Why don't you just come right out and say what you and everyone else was thinking tonight?' Jake demanded. 'She acted like a madwoman. Like someone deranged.'

'She's told me she's a. . .a friend,' Olivia murmured. 'It must have been a shock to see her, hear her talk to you like that.'

The dark head shook decisively. 'If the truth be known, I'm not sure how to handle her.' He glanced sideways at Olivia and added, 'She's more than just a friend.'

Olivia swallowed. 'A lover, then—'

'No!' There was violence in his tone. 'Not that! Never that!'

'But I thought—'

'Forget what you thought,' Jake replied sharply, turning to look at her. 'Just forget it, OK? It will be miles away from the truth, so just don't bother.'

'I'm going!' Olivia, hurt by Jake's angry tones, moved to go past him. So Sophie wasn't a lover at the moment, she thought; well, it could only be a matter of time. 'I should have left an hour ago, instead of wandering outside, wondering like a fool what was going on. Waiting for you, for. . .for this!'

'Don't leave.' Jake stepped in front of her and caught her arm as Olivia tried to move away. She pulled a little and felt the power and determination in his restraint. 'You're not going anywhere.'

She glared up into his face, half lit by the moonlight, half in shadow. 'If you think you can treat me like some stupid girl,' she cried, 'if you think I'm going to stick around to be—!'

But he wasn't listening.

Olivia gasped as the pressure of his body moved her back against the balustrade. She gripped the rough stone blindly, conscious of the intensity of his need, the erotic sensations that were flaring into life as his hands slid over her body, as he lowered his mouth to her lips in a kiss that was both insistent and intense.

'I have got to have you again!' he murmured huskily. 'That one thought has been torturing me all evening.' His mouth was warm on her neck. His lips grazed the softness of her skin as he whispered erotically into her ear. 'Let's make love, Olivia!' he drawled softly. 'I really want to feel you next to me.'

Images instantly filled Olivia's head. Images of the two of them together again. The whole idea of them as lovers, of taking and giving pure physical pleasure didn't seem outrageous when it came from this man's lips. Why? How could it be? The fact that he didn't care, that they hadn't formed any kind of solid relationship, didn't seem to matter. When he touched her and kissed her and held her, loving him made absolute sense.

The music from the ballroom was drifting on the

cool night air. Jake placed a gentle finger on her lips.
'Listen!'

It was a sensuous melody; moody and romantic. In
her dreams Olivia had imagined dancing under the
stars to such a tune.

He must have read her thoughts, because the fairy
tale was enacted once again. He pulled her close against
his body, wrapping her within the circle of his arms,
moving her slowly in time to the music.

'You know it's inevitable, don't you?' he informed
her steadily. 'There's no question that we'll continue to
be lovers.'

Olivia laid her head against the broad chest and
closed her eyes. She could smell the fresh masculine
scent of him, feel the sensual power of each purposeful
movement. Time stood still. Infinity beckoned. She had
never known such depth of feeling, such intense longing
for another human being.

Such a still, quiet night. Cool and crisp. Beautiful
music, beautiful movement. . .

As the music came to an end Jake lowered his head
and kissed Olivia's upturned mouth. Then he took her
by the hand and led her across the wide balcony.

'Where are we going?' Her voice was barely a
whisper as she gazed up at the strong profile.

'To a place I know. Away from here.' He moved
purposefully, leading Olivia down stone steps, around
the back of the house, then across a large paved area,
passing large urns and clipped hedges that were like
monsters in the moonlight.

'To the wood?' Olivia looked up in surprise as Jake
followed a narrow path that veered off to the right,
away from the house.

'Don't worry. It's not too far.' He stopped and

looked down at her. 'You'll like it. Now hold on. We don't want to ruin that beautiful dress.'

He lifted her into his arms and Olivia instinctively linked her fingers around his neck, feeling safe and secure against the strength of his body. She hadn't the first idea where he was taking her or what she would find on arrival but she didn't care.

She felt the thrill of erotic sensation as Jake paused to kiss her neck, hungry with need, with wanting her. This feeling of absolute certainty was a revelation. It had been missing for all of her life and now she had discovered its existence she wasn't about to let it slip away.

Jake Savage was her destiny and nothing could alter it.

# CHAPTER FIVE

THE moonlight led them to a clearing in the woods. The cottage was small and square, with two windows, a door and a chimney; Hansel and Gretal's cottage.

'Are the walls made of gingerbread?' Olivia asked as Jake swung open the gate.

'Not quite.' Two strides and they were at the door. He reached up to a ledge above and inserted the key he found into the lock. His eyes fell to her face. 'You think it's quaint?'

Olivia nodded. 'An unusual place. . .'

'For seduction?' Jake smiled and pushed open the door. 'A very private place,' he continued. 'We won't be disturbed here.'

He carried her into the room. There were thick rugs and stone walls and a large, comfortable-looking settee placed in front of a fireplace, where paper and sticks were already laid waiting.

'Two minutes.' He placed her down on the cream cushions. 'I'll light the fire.' He lowered his head and kissed her mouth very softly, very slowly, savouring the taste, dragging his lips away, looking deep into her eyes. 'It won't take long.'

Olivia gazed at the strong back, the broad shoulders, the dark, dark hair, watched as the flames burnt brightly, casting the man before her into sharp relief, and thought about the strength of her need. Where had such desire sprung from? How was it this man could ignite such feelings when other men—men she had known, respected and liked over the years—failed to do so?

'I won't regret this, will I?' Olivia murmured as Jake turned back towards her, as he slipped searching fingers beneath the straps of her dress, as his mouth tasted her skin, biting erotically at her flesh. She arched her neck as his hands travelled to her throat, as he held her head gently, dismantling her carefully formed chignon, running his hands through the long, silky strands of her hair. 'Jake!' His name was a breath on her lips. 'Tell me I won't regret this.'

'You won't regret it.' His voice was husky, thick with need. 'Think about how much you want me,' he drawled. 'Just relax and let me do the rest. . .'

He undressed her slowly, sliding the lilac silk away from her skin; ebony eyes travelled over her heated body, lingering on the white lace underwear. He kissed her again, touching her, so that the ache in Olivia's pelvis grew with each moment that passed, so that she clung to him, reaching up to remove his dinner jacket, watching, *feeling* the urgency in him as he wrenched away the bow tie and the white shirt, tossing each expensive item carelessly onto the floor.

His lovemaking was sensuously controlled, ruthlessly designed to bring maximum pleasure to them both. Olivia gasped in wonderment as erotic desire surged through her body. All these years, she thought, without realising that her body was capable of such intense sensation.

Jake loomed above her, strong and tanned and intensely male, watching her reactions to each new movement, each shocking touch. 'Are you ready?' he growled hoarsely. 'Do you want this?'

She nodded, unable to speak, arching her body, aching to feel him inside her.

'Say you want me!' he demanded. 'Tell me, Olivia. Leave me in no doubt!'

'I want you!' she cried wildly, clinging to him. 'Oh, yes, I want you!'

He took her then, and she cried out as the waves of feeling spiralled and surged within, as he brought her to the edge, prolonging the ecstasy, teasing and tormenting so that Olivia felt she'd die with wanting him.

'Jake!' It was a plea from the heart as the torment continued, and he responded accordingly, completing her ecstasy, bringing them both to the pinnacle of true physical fulfilment.

Afterwards there was a moment when he held her. A brief, intense hug that she prayed held some sort of meaning. Olivia stroked the dark hair and kissed the rough, angled cheek, savouring the seconds of closeness before he moved away.

Such a brief moment, but it meant so much. It gave her hope.

She wanted him to say something, but she hadn't a clue what. Now that their passion was spent she felt vulnerable again. It had been what she had wanted and yet there was still this feeling of emptiness and desolation. . .

'What are you thinking about?'

'Mmm?' He twisted around to look at her, his eyes drawn by her nakedness. He shook his head a little and then looked back at the flames. 'Nothing in particular.'

'Is. . .is it Sophie?' Olivia murmured. 'Are you worried about her?'

'Tell me about your life in London.'

Olivia hesitated. She wasn't prepared for the bluntness of his questioning. She took a breath, gulped and tried to work out how to answer. 'What do you want to know?'

He turned and looked back at her. 'You were in a relationship. Why did it end?'

'He walked away one day and married my secretary.'

'That's how, not why.'

Olivia wrapped her arms around her body, curling her legs up in front of her like a shield. 'We had just been going through the motions, I suppose,' she murmured flatly. 'He wanted to take. . .things further—'

'By things, I presume you mean sex?'

Olivia released a breath. 'Do you have to be so. . . so. . .'

'Straightforward?'

'. . .blunt?' Olivia finished firmly. 'Can't you see this is difficult enough for me as it is?'

'So you didn't want a physical relationship,' Jake continued as Olivia fell silent. 'Why?'

'Looking back, I can see that our relationship was pretty superficial,' Olivia murmured. 'We may have spent quite a lot of time together and we had a lot in common, because of our work, but we were never truly close. . .' Her voice trailed away and she shrugged to cover her unease, glancing at Jake's enigmatic expression.

'You weren't in love with him, then?' He was observing her closely, as if her answer was of vital importance. 'You weren't saving yourself so that you could be his virginal bride?'

Olivia took a breath and then shook her head firmly. 'No.'

'But it still hurt when he walked out on you?'

'Of course it did!' she replied swiftly. 'He betrayed

me, he betrayed my trust. He worked on the magazine too—he was the art director—and I had to carry on, enduring the staff's sympathy whilst Paul and my secretary honeymooned in Tahiti. Can you imagine how it *felt*?'

'So you ran away.'

'I didn't run away!' Olivia responded sharply. 'Paul's desertion just made me sit back and look at my life, that's all.'

'And you decided you didn't like what you saw?'

Olivia sighed. 'No.'

'I'm sorry.'

Was he? She looked at him and thought that yes, maybe he was. 'I don't care now,' she continued awkwardly. 'No, I don't, honestly,' she repeated, seeing his sceptical gaze. 'I had got trapped into a certain way of life. It was stifling me. I took a long, hard look at myself, at my life after Paul went, and found that underneath the gloss of modern-day living I wasn't enjoying myself, I wasn't happy.'

'And are you happy now?'

Olivia worked at schooling her expression. 'Do you mean generally, or right at this moment?' she murmured.

The ebony eyes regarded her steadily. 'Either. Both.' He gestured with his hands. 'Whatever.'

'I feel as if the possibility of happiness is within my reach,' Olivia replied carefully. 'You know, like a cake,' she added lightly; 'I've got all the ingredients at hand. . . I just need to find the right recipe now.'

She saw his mouth twist crookedly at her metaphoric description. 'I see.'

'And you?' she asked swiftly, grabbing the opportunity while it still pretented itself. 'Are you happy?'

Jake's dark brows drew together. 'I thought you'd already worked that one out for yourself,' he murmured. He turned from her suddenly and looked back at the flames flickering in the grate. 'You're way ahead of me on this one, Olivia,' he drawled. 'You've shopped, you have the ingredients.' She saw him shake his head. 'I don't even have a clue what it is I want to bake.'

Olivia reached out a hand and gently touched the smooth, bronzed back. 'I wish I could make you happy,' she ventured quietly.

He released a short, unamused laugh. 'It's a thankless task, Olivia. Many have tried and fallen by the wayside.'

He hadn't said she made him happy. Had she honestly expected him to? She frowned. No...no, she hadn't, not really. The fact that she experienced the most incredible feeling of joy whilst he was making love to her didn't make the slightest bit of difference. He felt one way, she felt another. She couldn't superimpose her rapture, however desperately she wanted to. 'Maybe they didn't try hard enough.'

'It's not worth the effort.' He turned back around to face her and his ebony eyes pierced her face. 'Believe me.'

'You're not made of stone,' Olivia whispered. 'In my experience no one is. When we made love —'

'Olivia! Leave it, please! Just accept that I'm made a certain way —'

'Like a clam that doesn't want to open up?' Olivia cut in swiftly.

The firm mouth curved of its own accord. 'If you like.'

Olivia took a breath. 'I just thought we could talk a

little, that's all,' she murmured, cursing herself for
pushing too far, too soon. 'After all, you showed an
interest in my relationship with Paul. Surely that
means—?'

'Please! Will you forget the amateur psychoanalysis,
Olivia?' Jake replied sharply. 'If I wanted medical help
I'd pay someone in Harley Street for the privilege!' He
rose from the sofa and walked towards a door in the
far corner of the room. He glanced back at Olivia's
pale face. 'I told you it wasn't worth the effort, didn't
I?' he added grimly. '*Now* do you believe me? I can be
a real bastard, Olivia,' he gritted. 'The sooner you
accept that fact, the better for both of us.'

She watched him leave the room. Then her misted
eyes fell to her clothes, which lay discarded on the
floor, and she began to dress, trying to fasten the lilac
silk with fingers that trembled.

The fact that she recognised his cruel anger as the
defensive mechanism it was didn't help the way she
felt. He *was* a bastard—a deliberate one at that. He
had hurt her. He would go on hurting her. He didn't
seem to enjoy doing it, but that was small comfort—he
did it all the same.

'Where are you going?'

She stood, half naked, clutching the lilac silk to her,
transfixed by his voice. She pursed her lips. 'Where do
you think?'

He had a towel slung low around his hips, two glasses
in his hands. 'You want to leave?'

'Yes!' She gulped, glaring at the sensationally attractive face, her eyes lingering on the finely moulded
mouth, the rich, dark eyes. 'No...' She found her
blonde head shaking. 'I... I don't know—'

'Come here.'

He expected her to obey. She recognised the strength of his command and wondered at her own weakness as she responded and slowly retraced her steps.

He took her chin urgently in his hand and looked down into her confused face. 'I'm sorry,' he murmured gruffly. 'I can't say I didn't mean to hurt you, because you know that I did, but I am sorry.' There was a brooding expression on his face. 'Do you regret our making love?' he demanded abruptly. 'Do you?'

Olivia swallowed and shook her head, clutching her dress against her lace bra. This man was so intense. So *deep*. She could feel the controlled power surging through his frame. 'No,' she whispered, meaning it. 'It was. . .' She struggled to finish the sentence. What words could adequately describe the way he had made her feel?

A dark brow was raised expressively. 'Good?'

It had been better than that—far better, but Olivia knew as she looked into the assured face that it would not be to her advantage ever to admit as much.

'Here!' Jake held out one of the glasses. 'Have some brandy. You look as if you need it.'

Hesitantly she accepted and took a cautious sip, choking a little as the fiery liquid hit the back of her throat.

His mouth curved sensuously. 'You're not used to it?' She shook her head. 'Are you cold?' He slipped his arms around Olivia's bare shoulders and drew her closer towards the fire. 'Sit here and have my jacket.' He tossed her lilac dress away and sat beside her on the floor, stretching his long legs out towards the flame. Olivia gripped the dinner jacket and held it close around her body. 'Don't frown.' He touched the lines on her forehead. 'It doesn't suit you. There's nothing to worry about.'

The lines deepened. 'Isn't there?'

'If it's the practicalities you're worrying about, don't. It was safe just now.' The mouth curved and his smile held warmth once again. 'Believe it or not but it's not in my nature to act irresponsibly.' He shook his head and looked at the flames thoughtfully. 'Never irresponsible,' he murmured, half to himself. 'Never that.'

'I hadn't even thought of it,' Olivia confessed quietly, watching the strong profile with some confusion. 'Thank you,' she murmured awkwardly.

'My pleasure.' His eyes were back on her face and her body. She felt reaction stir within as ebony eyes became predatory again, sweeping the length of her, lingering appreciatively on her slim, tanned legs, from her painted pink toenails to her slender calves, to her thighs, the curve of her hips, beyond...

'This isn't another one-night stand,' he murmured. 'You know that, don't you?'

Olivia felt her heartbeat quicken. 'I...' She hesitated.

'We're good together—physically,' Jake added swiftly. 'You know I want this to be a regular thing.'

Olivia stared at the flames. 'What about Sophie?'

He frowned and Olivia heard him curse softly beneath his breath. 'What about her?'

Anger flared as she looked back into the far too handsome face. 'Oh, nothing!' she cried wildly. 'It's perfectly straightforward, isn't it?' She flashed him a look. 'Well, for you it might be! You probably indulge in this sort of thing all of the time. But it's clear from what Sophie said—'

'What did she say?' His voice was curt, the question sharp as Olivia's voice fell away.

'Nothing. It. . .it doesn't matter.'

'Clearly it does.' He glared at her. 'Look, it's important you understand that Sophie and I have known each other since we were kids. She's been through a rough time. She has no close family of her own and now that. . .' He paused and Olivia sensed a change of tone. 'Now that my family have gone too she looks to me for emotional support.'

'Gone?' Olivia frowned.

He regarded her steadily. 'Yes.'

'What do you mean—gone?'

'Exactly what I say; my family were wiped out in an air crash a couple of years ago.'

'Oh!' Olivia's eyes glittered with sudden tears. For a long moment she hadn't a clue what to say. Eventually she managed to murmur the standard reply that sounded totally inadequate in the circumstances. 'I'm. . . I'm so sorry.'

Dark brows narrowed as he stared at her wide-eyed dismay. 'Are you?' Jake gave a short laugh. 'That's nice.'

'Don't!'

He turned to look at her. 'Don't what?'

'You know what I'm talking about!' Olivia's voice hardened to match his expression. 'I'm not a punch bag!' she flared, scrambling to her feet. 'And I won't be used like one. I'm not here to soak up your verbal aggression! Use somebody else, some*thing* else if you want a means of releasing your physical tensions!'

'Olivia! Don't go!' He reached up and placed a hand on her body. 'You're right. I'm giving you hell and you don't deserve any of it.' His fingers curled around her wrist and he pulled her gently back towards him. 'Forget the way I spoke just now.' Jake kissed her mouth, briefly at first and then again, his lips lingering and searching as if tasting her was all he could think about, as if he could draw strength from the warmth and intensity of their kiss.

When he finally released her he seemed to struggle with some inner conflict for a moment as he met her gaze, and then he spoke in a cool, matter-of-fact tone. 'The plane was flying over the Atlantic Ocean; my family was on board. One engine failed, the other caught fire.' He glanced towards the flames shimmering in front of them. 'It crashed.' His voice became hard. 'All one hundred and seventy people died, my family included. End of story.'

She wanted to cry; for Jake, for his family, for everyone involved in the tragedy. She moved closer to him, linking her arms around his neck, pressing her cheek against his, feeling the rigidity of his frame, feeling the hurt. 'If ever you feel the need to talk—'

'I won't!' His voice was flat. 'You'll have to understand that. It's an integral part of any...arrangement we may come to. No questions. No probing. My family is dead and gone; no amount of talking will bring them back.'

'But it might help you,' Olivia replied. 'You're suffering still, I can see that—'

'Maybe I am.' The hard mouth curved. 'OK, so there's no maybe about it.' He flashed her a look. 'I want you to forget all about it, Olivia. I don't go in for introspection.'

She watched him in silence for a moment, struggling to keep her control. 'Why are you being like this?'

'Like what?'

'Do you think it's a sign of weakness...to show emotion? Is that it?' Olivia asked quietly.

'What the hell does that matter? It's the way I am!' His expression was fierce all at once. 'Understand and accept it, Olivia, because I'm not about to change.'

'And if I don't want to?'

His mouth tightened ominously. 'Then it's the end. Our relationship will have run its course.'

'You really are a cold-hearted swine!' Olivia started to get to her feet, but Jake reached out and held her by the arm. 'Let me go!' she flared. 'You think I would want to—'

He tugged her sharply and she fell against his chest. Her hands splayed out against the bronzed skin with its curl of dark hair and then he was kissing her again, hungrily, passionately, deeply. 'You're not going anywhere,' he growled. His hands pushed the dinner jacket from her shoulders. 'We both know that...'

Endless love. Endless pleasure. When the dawn broke it was beautiful. Sunlight shone into the cottage and Olivia opened her eyes to find herself lying on the deep, wide sofa with a blanket over her.

She got up and padded over to the window, wrapping the soft wool close around her naked body, watching as the sunlight filtered slowly through the trees as the early-morning mist moved and swirled through the tangle of branches in the wood.

'Good. You're awake. Do you want some breakfast?'

She looked up. Jake looked rugged and incredibly sexy, dressed in evening attire that looked out of place on this bright spring morning. A growth of beard shaded his jaw, no tie, tousled hair... Olivia felt her stomach tighten and took a hasty breath. Was this her destiny? This emptiness? In her dreams he loved her. In her dreams he wanted more than just sex. . .

'Olivia?' He ruffled her hair and his mouth curved attractively. 'You're miles away. What are you thinking about?'

'Me?' She glanced into his face, then back at the trees, listening to the chirpy chorus of bird song. 'I wasn't thinking of anything in particular.' She let out a long sigh. 'Just experiencing, just feeling. It's beautiful, isn't it?'

He looked out at the wood. 'Sure is.'

'Can we take the long way back?'

Jake shook his head. 'Sorry. I'm on call today. I should have been home an hour ago.'

'But it's Sunday!' Olivia heard the disappointment in her voice and cursed silently. Go on, she told herself crossly, make yourself look a total fool! Give him all the wrong signals; start acting like a clinging woman without a life of your own!

'Unfortunately animals don't fall sick to order,' he drawled. 'Believe me, life would be a lot simpler if they did.'

'But you have a colleague, don't you?' Olivia queried.

'Yes. But he's worked hard all week. And he has a family. His wife and three daughters barely see enough of him as it is. It's my practice, and I have to pull my weight.'

'Yes.' Olivia forced a smile. 'Yes, of course you do. I understand.'

Dark eyes rested on her face, then he kissed her mouth. 'Good. Now, you can stay here for a while if you like, or you can get dressed and leave with me. It's your choice.'

Olivia shivered at his touch and tried to combat the reaction with a voice that sounded casual. 'I'd like to see more of the wood,' she murmured. 'The bluebells are wonderful.'

'Get dressed, then. If you hurry I'll show you a way that will bring you out onto the footpath near Honeysuckle Cottage.' He glanced at his wrist-watch, then reached for Olivia's clothes and handed them to her.

She dressed swiftly, hugging her velvet wrap close over her lilac gown. 'Have you got everything?' Jake had been standing before the window whilst Olivia made herself decent, and on seeing she was ready he opened the cottage door.

Olivia nodded and tried to look as controlled and businesslike as her lover. 'Yes.'

'Good.' He glanced across at her as the door of the cottage was shut with a bang and the key replaced. 'You'll be OK?'

'Of course!' Olivia forced an uncaring smile. 'Why shouldn't I be?'

He shrugged and raised dark brows. 'No reason. The path's over there.' He gestured away towards Olivia's left. 'It's clearly marked. You should have no problem finding your way home.'

She looked into his face and caught the end of a lingering gaze. 'Thanks.'

'I'll call you.' He began walking away from her, down another path that led in the direction of the impressive mansion, which was just visible through the misted trees. 'Soon,' he added, turning back as he looped his jacket over his shoulder. 'You can count on it.'

# CHAPTER SIX

THE walk through the woods might have been wonderful, but Olivia had hardly been aware of it. She had been home, she had bathed and changed. She had tried to concentrate on any number of useful tasks—around the cottage, in the garden and the orchard—all to no avail. After a couple of hours she could bear it no longer. Sunday was usually considered to be a day of rest, but today Olivia knew she would get no peace.

Not after last night.

The peal of church bells greeted her on arrival at the village. Olivia paused and looked up at the tall grey spire that rose majestically into the azure sky. She waited until the congregation, which was just emerging from the morning service, had dispersed and then she crossed the village street, opened the lych-gate and ventured into the churchyard.

Jake Savage. These obsessive feelings she had for him weren't just because of lust and desire. Walking back alone through the woodland early this morning had somehow helped to crystalise her feelings. The beauty of the place, with its thick swath of bluebells, like a carpet at her feet, and the verdant greenery all around had helped to bring everything into a sharp and vivid focus.

She loved him. She didn't *want* to love him—Olivia recognised emotional suicide when it hit her in the face—but there wasn't anything she could do about it. Or was there?

The churchyard had a large wild area, with head-stones dating back several hundreds of years. The gravestones here were simple or ornate depending on the wealth of the family concerned, the stone crusty and covered in lichens, the grass overgrown and unkempt. Olivia lingered here for a long while, reading the inscriptions, strolling through the dappled shade, experiencing the familiar feelings that always came to the fore when she entered such a place; an impressive sense of history and time passing and her own fragile mortality.

Maybe it wasn't so clever coming in here. A melan-choly, quite deep and profound, was beginning to assail her. Too sensitive, that was her trouble. Too full of emotion. Too fragile after the events of last night.

She sat down on a bench, and leant wearily against the little brass plaque commemorating someone's exist-ence. It was warm and she felt tired. The newer graves were at the far end of the churchyard. In a moment she would get up and search. Jake's family had been killed and for that reason this quiet place meant something to him—she wanted it to mean something to her.

It had come to this. Names, dates, snippets of infor-mation, anything that would bring her a little closer to the man she loved.

Olivia heard the noisy squeak of the lych-gate and cursed the fact that she would not be alone. She moved along the bench to see who it was. If it was a villager, someone who was at the ball last night, then she would slip away unnoticed; she knew where any conversation would eventually end up—Sophie Carlton's outburst would be the talk of the village for a few more days yet. . .

Her heart thudded violently in her chest, her

thoughts skidded to a halt. Even from this distance Jake looked magnificent. Olivia forgot to breathe, watching as he made his way towards the area of the churchyard that was newer, and fresher. He wore dark glasses against the glare of the sun, pale chinos, a casual shirt that was undone at the throat...and he was carrying a bouquet of flowers.

Olivia, gripped by a mixture of fascination at the coincidence of such a meeting and real dread at being discovered, watched as he stood immobile for a long while, staring at one particular headstone, before crouching down to remove the faded blooms with slow deliberation.

Suddenly she didn't want to be here. She didn't want to see any of this. It was private. And anyway, there was self-preservation to consider; some deep instinct told her that Jake would be extremely angry if he found her here.

She rose cautiously from the bench. She was wearing navy shorts and a striped nautical-style top, a crisp, sharp outfit that wasn't exactly an aid to her camouflage. Would he see her? Maybe not. Jake seemed intent on his task and if she kept her movements smooth and silent Olivia felt there was a chance she would get away unnoticed.

She was wrong. He looked up as she made her move, staring intently down the long, wide green path, transfixing her with the power of his presence, even at this distance.

They stared at each other for what felt like eternity. Then slowly Olivia walked towards him, her heart thudding painfully in her chest. She felt like a rabbit caught in the glare of a beam. The intensity of his gaze didn't alter and he reeled her in, slowly, relentlessly.

He got to his feet as she approached, towering above her, hands thrust into trouser pockets; a dark, dangerous stranger who just happened to be her lover.

'Small world.'

He was angry—very angry.

Olivia felt a shiver run through her, even though the sun was warm on her back. 'Yes.' To her immense surprise, her voice sounded reasonably firm, despite the multitude of heavy-footed butterflies that were churning her stomach into a mass of apprehension. 'It's. . .a beautiful churchyard,' she added, dragging her gaze away from the rugged face. 'I popped in. . .on. . . on the spur of the moment to take a look around. . .' Not sounding so good now; she was gabbling and her voice sounded weak and more unsure with each jerkily uttered syllable.

'Oh, yes?' Slowly he removed his dark glasses, but the cold, dark gaze didn't tell her a thing.

Did he believe her? She doubted it very much. 'I saw the sign on my way in—about the bad state of the church roof,' she added, forcing herself to continue, to say *something*. 'I'd. . . I'd really like to help in some way.'

'Are you a churchgoer?'

'No, but—'

'Well, why help, then?' His voice was rough, cutting across Olivia's half-spoken sentence. 'You're new to the village, the church has been here hundreds of years. I'm surprised you want to make it a concern of yours!'

Olivia stared at the hard features for a moment in silence, debating whether to turn around now and walk away, or battle on. She opted, foolishly, she knew, for the latter. 'Nevertheless,' she continued, forcing her voice to sound light, 'I think I'll lend my services to the cause. I do have some skills that may be of use.'

'Oh, yes?' There was a chilling lack of emotion in his tone, a sharp, sarcastic twist of the mouth that made Olivia's face flame with anger and embarrassment.

'I'm talking about my executive experience!' she flashed. 'I used to run one of the most prestigious fashion magazines in the country.'

'And you think that's relevant?' He threw her a scornful look.

'Why shouldn't it be?' She felt despair growing inside. They were talking like strangers—no, worse than that; like hated enemies. Was it always going to be this way? 'I'm good at organising. I have contacts that might be useful.'

The attractive mouth twisted derisively. 'You know a firm that can supply fifteenth-century roof tiles on the cheap?' The dark eyes surveyed her without expression. He looked cold. Cold and hard and ruthless. 'What are you really doing here, Olivia? Following me? Spying?'

'No!' This couldn't be her lover of the previous evening, Olivia thought miserably. This unsmiling man bore no resemblance to the sensuous individual who had borne her away on a rising tide of ecstasy. There had been warmth and immense passion. He *had* wanted her. A vision of the two of them flashed into her mind, making her heartbeat quicken. She saw Jake release a taut breath and wondered if he had been thinking about their lovemaking too.

'Well, what, then?'

'I. . . I just wanted a look around,' Olivia murmured weakly.

'You think I'm stupid? I tell you about my parents'

death and then surprise, surprise, next thing I find you in the graveyard!'

'Please... Jake...' Olivia met the hard gaze with eyes that glistened. 'Isn't there something I can say to stop you treating me like this?'

He looked down into her face. 'I don't know what you're talking about.'

'Don't you?' she prompted unsteadily.

'For God's sake!' he grated, throwing the bouquet he was holding angrily to the ground. 'Don't start getting emotional!'

'Why?' Olivia swallowed back the lump in her throat. 'Isn't emotion allowed? Is that another requirement of our relationship?'

'Yes!' He turned from her and began picking up the dead flowers that lay beside the grave. 'I don't want you here!' he added roughly. 'Can't you see that? It's the last place I expected to find you. Just go! Look at the church roof or something!'

'Damn you!' Olivia spun towards him and gripped hold of his shirt. 'Don't you turn away from me! How can you treat me like this? How can you be so cold and heartless and hateful?'

'Because it's the best way.' His eyes were like fire, burning into her, scorching her very soul. 'I'm not about to open up to you, Olivia. Once, just once, I made the foolish mistake of allowing someone to get close.' He surveyed her with grim self-control. 'Never again. This is the way I am. Don't you dare start believing that you can change me, or change the way I choose to feel!'

Her fingers slid from his shirt. Touching him was torture. Being near to him meant wanting him. She took a step back as if she had been physically struck.

Her eyes latched angrily on to the hard, rigid lines of his face, on to the derisive twist of his cruel mouth.

'We share one common bond Olivia, just one,' he gritted, 'an insatiable need to have sex with one another. Don't complicate that, don't start confusing it with anything else.'

'You swine!' Without thinking, Olivia raised her hand and lashed out fiercely. There was a sharp sound as her hand met his jaw. She felt a stinging along her fingers and gasped as the realisation of what she had done struck home.

There was a long, painful silence.

'Did that make you feel any better?'

'I'm. . . I'm not sorry.' Olivia's voice was shaking like a leaf. 'You deserved it!'

She tried to turn away, but Jake flicked out a hand and caught her wrist. 'I know I did.' He released an unsteady breath. Then he swore and the cold, hard, mask slipped for a fraction of a second. 'I know!' He shook his head in something approaching despair. 'I apologise for what I said just now. I—'

'Don't waste your breath!' Olivia's brows snapped together. 'We both know you meant it.' She looked away and found her gaze drawn inexorably towards Jake's family gravestone. 'Your *brother*?' Her blue eyes scanned the inscription swiftly. 'He died in the crash too?' Olivia looked quickly back at Jake. 'I didn't realise.'

'Why should you?' Dark eyes pierced hers. 'I didn't tell you.'

'Jake. . .' She controlled the quiver in her voice. 'Let me help!'

'You can bring them back, can you?' he demanded urgently. 'You can put right all my mistakes?'

'What mistakes?'

There was a long pause. He seemed to be fighting himself, fighting whatever thoughts were running around in his mind. 'Why don't you simply accept the fact that I'm not interested in sharing my innermost secrets with you, Olivia?' he demanded. 'It will save us both a lot of wasted energy.'

'But you still expect me to sleep with you!'

He gazed down at her. Every part of him exuded energy and strength and masculine force. 'I don't *expect* you to do anything,' he replied crisply. 'You're a grown woman with a mind of your own. You will do as you please.' His gaze hardened. 'Or are you trying to imply that what you've done so far has been against your will?'

Olivia flushed angrily. 'Damn you!' she cried unsteadily. 'You are such a callous swine!'

'You think I don't know that?' he stated flatly. 'It's been said before.'

'By your family?' Olivia flashed, wanting to hurt him as much as he was hurting her.

'Amongst others, yes.'

The words were spoken and she couldn't take them back. Olivia stared miserably into Jake's hardened face and watched as his ebony eyes narrowed until they were like chips of granite.

'I'm sorry!' Olivia placed her hand to her mouth. 'I shouldn't. . . I shouldn't have said that. I didn't mean—' She shook her head as emotion overwhelmed her suddenly. She closed her eyes to cover the tears then turned from him as they spilled over onto her cheeks, and ran at full pelt along the grassy path towards the lych-gate.

He came after her. She hadn't expected that. She

wasn't sure she wanted it. After all, she deserved to be punished for saying such a wicked thing. Maybe it would be best if her torment ended here.

'Olivia!'

She halted just before she reached the gate. Her fingers gripped the wood. Her heart was pounding in her chest; she felt sick and giddy and distraught. It took great effort to keep upright as she waited for him.

'Don't run away. Where the hell do you think you're going?'

Olivia hung her head 'I. . . I don't know.'

'You think I would let you go like this?'

She wiped at the wetness on her cheeks. 'It's. . . probably best. Jake, I didn't mean to be so. . .hurtful.'

'I deserved it. I had a taste of my own medicine for a change. Here. Dry your eyes.' He handed over a large white handkerchief, watching impassively as she took it to scrub at her tears. 'You look pale,' he murmured, tilting her chin with one strong finger. 'Do you feel OK? You look as if you're about to faint.'

'I. . . I feel a little light-headed, that's all,' Olivia admitted quietly. She tried to cope as her legs began to buckle, right on cue beneath her. 'It's very warm, isn't it? I'll be OK,' she murmured anxiously as Jake's hands came around her body to support her. 'Let me go,' she croaked, hating that she should still be affected by his touch. 'I'm fine.'

'No, you're not.' Lean fingers smoothed back the silky blonde strands from her face. 'You look dreadful.'

'I haven't eaten since yesterday. I. . . I was going to get some lunch at the pub,' she murmured.

He shook his head. 'Not there. The food is lousy; the landlord is single and hasn't a clue about anything other than real ale. You can come back to my place and eat with me.'

'No.' Olivia shook her head determinedly. 'No.'

His voice was deceptively mild. 'It wasn't a request.'

She glanced up. 'You can't order me around! Just because. . .' she faltered and swallowed, fighting back the tears again '. . .we were together last night,' she croaked, 'it doesn't give you the right to—Oh!'

Her words were like fuel to a flame. Jake dragged her towards his hard body, crushing her within his arms. 'It gives me every right,' he asserted huskily. 'Lunch, with me.' He kissed her mouth firmly. 'No argument.'

She wasn't capable of replying. He saw that and took advantage of it, lifting her clear from the ground, carrying her through the gate and out onto the narrow village street. Olivia made one final effort to pull herself together as he set her back onto her feet and opened the passenger door of the Range Rover, parked near by.

'I feel fine now,' she murmured. 'There really is no need for this. . .'

He wasn't interested. Dark eyes met hers as he held open the door and, after a brief pause, Olivia got in without a word.

The mansion looked just as impressive by day. The Range Rover was brought to a halt at the front steps and they both got out.

'Are you sure your housekeeper won't mind my staying to lunch?' Olivia queried as she jumped down from the vehicle. Stupid question; she saw that immediately. Jake Savage was lord and master of all he surveyed, and he didn't even bother to answer.

'You can wash through there.' He pointed fleetingly in the direction of a corridor that led off the panelled hallway. 'I'll be in the study.'

He left her standing and walked towards a half-opened door on the right. Olivia caught a glimpse of a sombre book-lined room that could have, *should* have been delightful, if the long, dark red velvet curtains had been drawn back a little further and the sun had been allowed to stream in through the well-proportioned windows.

She stood uncertainly for a moment and then took the route he had indicated. There were many doors at regular intervals along the wide corridor and she hadn't a clue which one he had meant. Olivia turned the handle of the first rather cautiously and peered inside. Gloom. She glanced towards the window and saw that the curtains in the large square room were fully drawn, precluding the light. There were dust sheets covering several items of bulky furniture, a slight stale smell that told her immediately that the room hadn't been used in a long time.

The next door, on the opposite side, was pretty much the same, covered in dust, shrouded with sheets that prevented prying eyes. There was an Adam fireplace and many pictures here, too, hung on fine hand-printed wallpaper that surely dated back many, many years. Olivia hesitated and then took a step inside. The windows were tall and wide. Cautiously she began to cross the floor, keeping her feet to the edges of the room to avoid treading on the expensive-looking rug.

'What do you think you're doing?'

Olivia jumped dramatically. She felt her heart thud with the shock and spun around to face Jake. 'Did you have to do that?' she demanded shakily. 'You frightened the life out of me!'

'Were you looking for something in particular?' His expression was hard again. 'Or just generally prying?'

Olivia swallowed, hating the fact that he was making her feel like a potential thief. 'I didn't know which room,' she told him stiffly. 'You said along here, but there are so many doors—'

'And what were you trying to do—exit through the window?'

'N. . .no, I just wanted to look out. . .to let in a little light, and. . .get my bearings,' Olivia added, knowing the lie uttered so desperately would never be believed.

'As you can very well see, these rooms aren't in use,' he informed her sharply. 'Now, if you don't mind. . .!' He took her by the arm, shutting the door firmly behind them both, and guided her back along the corridor. 'You'll find the cloakroom is here.' He indicated a door that was just off the hallway and half hidden by an impressive piece of sculpture.

'I wasn't being nosy!' Olivia insisted, conscious of the unflinching gaze. 'There's no need to look at me as if I'm an intruder who's just tried to run away with the family silver! Goodness, Jake, I was only looking; they are such grand rooms, after all—'

'If I wanted those rooms admired,' he drawled, 'I'd have signs showing the way and a man on the door selling tickets!' He released a breath. 'Now freshen yourself up and then come and have a drink with me.'

'You know, it's not such a bad idea,' Olivia murmured thoughtfully on her return from the cloakroom.

Jake turned towards her, frowning slightly. 'What isn't?'

'You could sell tickets,' she announced. 'You could open parts of your house to the public.'

He looked at her as if she were mad. 'And why on earth would I want to do that?'

'To help the community, *your* community. To help fund the cost of the church roof.'

The hard mouth twisted derisively. 'Don't be ridiculous, Olivia. Just save your breath and have a drink.'

'I'm serious, Jake!' Olivia smiled encouragingly, enthused by the prospect. 'Can't you see what a great idea it is?'

'No, I cannot!' He threw her a vexed look. 'The whole thing would be a nightmare from start to finish.'

'Not if it was organised properly.'

'Olivia, you don't know what you're saying—'

'I do. I'm talking about the church roof. About a way of helping to boost the funds. Can't you even listen?' she demanded, irritation growing as Jake walked back towards the drawing-room. 'It's a good idea!'

'Maybe it is,' Jake drawled, 'but only if it concerns a different person. Only if it involves opening up someone else's house to hundreds of pairs of prying eyes.'

'There's no other house like this in the area. You know—'

'Didn't you hear what I said?' He wheeled around suddenly. 'Let it drop, for heaven's sake!'

There was a pause whilst Olivia struggled to control her temper and her emotions; she had felt the stirrings of real excitement, her marketing and business brain racing ahead to view the possibilities. If it had been anyone else, any other normal, more receptive human being, she thought angrily, they'd at least listen! 'It's a good idea,' she muttered stubbornly, repeating herself like a child who refused to recognise defeat. 'I know it is!'

Jake threw her a warning glance before holding out a glass of wine, and she fell silent, taking it from him, her mind still dwelling on the possibilities.

'I'm going to turn the orchard of Honeysuckle Cottage into a tea garden as soon as the house is fixed up,' she murmured quietly, moving to stand before the tall windows, drawing back the long velvet curtains with determination to allow the spring sunshine to stream in. 'I figured the footpath from the village would entice a lot of people my way. It's part of a well-known walk, isn't it?' she added, turning to look at Jake, who seemed lost, deep in thought, oblivious to what she was saying.

'Sorry?' He looked across and after a moment came and joined Olivia by the window. 'What did you say?'

'Honeysuckle Cottage,' Olivia repeated patiently. 'I want to turn the orchard into a tea garden. It would make a good stop-off point. The walk from the village skirts around my place and on to here, then loops back again.'

'That's right.' His eyes scanned her face for a moment. 'You hope to make a living doing that?'

'No, no, of course not. Well, not entirely,' Olivia amended. She hesitated for a moment, trying to decide whether or not to reveal all her ideas in one fell swoop, uncertain whether Jake would be even vaguely interested in what she had to say after the run-in of a few moments ago. 'I plan to open a junk shop in one of the barns,' she murmured cautiously. 'Old bric-à-brac, furniture that can be painted and done up in a country style, that sort of thing. No cheap foreign imports. Nothing tacky,' she added hastily.

The firm mouth curved in amusement. It was the first and only smile of the day so far and Olivia's stomach flipped over at the sight of it. 'Perish the thought,' he drawled. 'We both know you have far too much style for anything like that.'

'There's no need to patronise,' Olivia flared, her pleasure fading instantly. 'Or make fun. I told you because I thought you might be vaguely interested—I should have known better, of course!'

'I am interested and I wasn't being patronising,' Jake replied smoothly, 'or not intentionally, anyway.' He studied her face. 'I honestly think it's an excellent idea.'

'Really?' His positive response caught her off guard and Olivia's sapphire eyes lit up with immediate pleasure. 'Truthfully?'

Dark eyes gleamed across at her. He leant forward and kissed her briefly on the mouth. 'Cross my heart and hope to die!' He finished his drink and added, 'Actually, there may even be the odd thing lying around here that I have no use for. If I find anything I could pass it over for you to sell. The profits could go towards the church roof, couldn't they? How's that for compromise?'

'Oh, yes!' Olivia beamed and felt the hated tension that had been building between them fall away. 'That's a wonderful idea. Not as good as my one where you open your house,' she added daringly, 'but nearly as good!'

The well-shaped mouth curled. 'Were you this determined in London?' he enquired. 'Did you always get your own way?'

She met his gaze and felt her heart give another leap. 'Always.'

Ebony eyes gleamed. 'Not many people stood a chance, then, did they?'

'No.' Olivia smiled. 'Of course, I listened to other people's opinion,' she added, 'a good editor always does that, but when I set my heart on a course of action I was very rarely deflected from it.'

'We have something in common, then,' Jake drawled. He allowed his gaze to travel speculatively over the curves of her body, leaving her in no doubt as to where his thoughts lay. 'It seems we're two of a kind. When we've decided we want something we make sure we get it.' Dark eyes gleamed. 'Isn't that the case?'

Olivia had been holding her breath. Now she released it very softly, very slowly, conscious of another sort of tension that was building between them with ever-increasing speed. 'Yes.'

The sound of a gong shattered the silence suddenly. Jake raised his drink to his lips and drained the contents. 'Luncheon is served,' he announced with a wry smile. 'Let's eat. And then I have a few suggestions on how we spend the rest of the afternoon.'

# CHAPTER SEVEN

TALKING during the meal was out of the question; Jake ate in silence, preoccupied by thoughts that Olivia couldn't even begin to guess at.

The insistent bleep of his phone went off not long after a traditional dessert of flaky apple pie and cream had been served. Olivia glanced across, spoon halfway to her mouth, and watched as Jake, excusing himself, flipped back the cellular phone and listened intently to the voice at the other end.

'I have to go.' He pushed away the untouched dish and stood up, throwing his napkin down onto the long, polished oak table that dominated the sombre dining-room. 'There's an old lady in the village who owns at least twenty cats—one of them has just dragged itself back home, half mangled by a car.'

Olivia put down her spoon. 'Could. . .could I come?' she asked hopefully. 'I wouldn't get in the way,' she added, seeing the sceptical look in the ebony eyes. 'Honestly. And. . . I might be able to help.'

'I doubt that.' Jake moved away from the table. 'I'll just get my bag. I don't know how long I'll be—'

'Please!' Olivia followed him to the door. She looked up into his face and saw that his mind was already on the task ahead. 'Let me come.'

He frowned, glancing disbelievingly at Olivia's fervent expression. 'What on earth do you want to come for? It will be a messy, emotional scene—if you're looking for excitement and glamour, forget it. Mrs Wood is a mad old bird, there are cats everywhere—'

'I don't care,' Olivia interrupted firmly. 'I still want to come.' She hesitated, seeing that he still wasn't convinced. 'I really am interested. You see. . . I wanted to be a vet when I was a little girl,' she added self-consciously. 'I suppose deep down that desire's never gone away.'

Jake lifted his shoulders in a casual shrug. 'OK, you can tag along,' he replied, 'but don't say during or afterwards that I didn't warn you.'

Olivia followed close on his heels. He paused to pick up his veterinary bag from a side-table in the hall, scanned its contents thoroughly, snapped it shut and then marched outside, heading towards the Range Rover at a brisk pace, so that Olivia had to run to keep up.

'So, from vet to fashion-magazine editor,' he drawled as he skilfully manoeuvred the vehicle at speed through the lanes that led to the old woman's cottage. 'Quite a turn-around. What happened? Did you become more interested in clothes than the welfare of animals?'

'No.' Olivia ignored the derisive tone of his voice. 'The realities of life took over—at five you think you can do anything; by the time you reach the age of fifteen you realise you have certain limitations.' She looked sideways at the handsome profile. 'I just wasn't clever enough,' she added simply.

'You're honest at least,' Jake drawled. 'Although a great deal of it is down to hard work and determination—not that I don't think you have those qualities in abundance, of course,' he added with a curve of his mouth.

'Oh, I didn't—not at that age,' Olivia replied. 'Seven years' training to be a vet? It seemed like a lifetime.'

'It *felt* like a lifetime,' Jake responded drily.

'It. . .it was something you always wanted to do?' She had to ask. There was so much she wanted to know about him. So much.

'Yes. You could say it was a boyhood dream,' he remarked flatly. 'We had a lot of animals on the estate in those days when my parents were alive. There was a farm and extensive stables. I spent practically every waking hour around cows, pigs or horses. My mother and father quite despaired of me.'

'And your brother? Was he interested?'

'Edward?' Jake shook his head. 'No. He was destined for other things.'

Olivia looked out of the passenger window, caught a glimpse of primroses on a sunny bank and decided to push on. 'Were you close?'

'Edward and I?' Jake shrugged. 'We were as different as chalk and cheese, but surprisingly we got along fine.'

'And your parents?'

'What about my parents?'

Olivia hesitated a fraction; she could see the defensive shield being erected before her very eyes. 'Were you close to them?'

'Not particularly,' he replied shortly. 'In the end. . . I felt I hardly knew them.' His tone was brisk as he drew the vehicle to a halt outside a striking black and white cottage and turned off the ignition. 'Here we are.'

No more questions, Olivia thought, watching the closed profile. Definitely no more answers.

Jake reached for his bag, opened the driver's door and got out. 'I suggest you watch where you stand and where you sit,' he remarked, glancing pointedly at Olivia's navy and white outfit as she followed him through the jungle of greenery that presumably once upon a time had been a garden. 'Mrs Wood's cats are everywhere.'

Inside was as Jake had intimated; cats and yet more cats.

Jake greeted Mrs Wood kindly, almost as if she was an old friend, introduced Olivia briskly and followed the woman, who looked pale and drawn and intensely worried, into a living-room where a fire was burning, even though it was sunny and warm outside.

On a rug, a towel placed carefully beneath him, was the poor, wretched cat. Jake bent down to examine the animal immediately. Olivia felt her heart sink—it looked pretty dead even to her untrained eye.

A moment later Jake looked up. 'I'm sorry,' he murmured, in a voice so gentle that Olivia hardly recognised it, 'but he's dead. Paxton, wasn't it?' He lifted the towel and began wrapping it round the body, so that none of them would have to look at the poor thing a moment longer. 'His injuries were very severe,' he added as the woman slumped miserably into a sagging chair. 'It will have been a blessed release. Even an animal half his age couldn't have coped with such severe internal injuries. It's a miracle he made it back home.' Jake glanced over and caught Olivia's eye. 'Let my friend make you a cup of tea. Whilst she's doing that I can bury Paxton in the garden for you.'

He lifted the cat into his arms and walked out of the room. Olivia followed, an anxious frown creasing her forehead. 'The kitchen's through here.' Jake indicated the door with a nod. 'She likes lots of sugar. Make us both one as well. And talk to her!'

Olivia frowned as he pushed open the door. 'But what shall I say?'

'Anything. It doesn't matter what you say, just keep her company. Show an interest.'

'But. . . I don't know her and—'

'Don't argue, just do it!' he ordered firmly. 'She needs a bit of company. Can't you see that?'

Olivia filled the kettle and waited apprehensively for it to boil. After five minute spent wondering what to say on her return to the other room she noticed she hadn't flicked the switch by the plug. Jake returned just as Olivia was pouring hot water over the teabags.

'Have you been in to see she's all right?' he asked as he removed several items of crockery from the sink and began washing his hands.

'No, not yet,' Olivia murmured. 'I kept thinking about that poor cat and—'

'Is that the only thing that's important to you?' Jake demanded in a low voice that held an edge of disgust. 'Don't you care about that old woman in there?'

'Of course I care!' Olivia retorted. 'Of course I do! But. . .but this is a new situation for me,' she added feebly. 'I wasn't sure how to handle it.'

Jake glanced around the cluttered kitchen. 'This is all rather too much of a contrast for the high-fashion guru, I suppose?'

'There's no need to mock!' Olivia flashed.

'I warned you it wouldn't be particularly pleasant,' Jake replied grimly. 'You didn't want to listen.'

Olivia turned her back away from the infuriating features, hating the fact that he was right. She shouldn't have come. From the very first moment she had felt out of place, out of her depth, a total contrast to Jake, who seemed to know exactly what to do, what to say. . .

She picked up two of the mugs. 'The tea's ready,' she declared stiffly. 'I've left yours on the draining board.'

'You're a good lad!' The old woman smiled gratefully up at Jake as he struggled to find a place to sit down. 'And you're his girl?' The woman smiled faintly at Olivia. 'About time Jake found someone,' she declared. 'Not been a good couple of years for you, has it, my lad? First one thing and then another. Course, I never could take to his father, you know. Always coming along, bossing me about, telling me how I ought to live my life. Jake's not like that, for all his smart ways, are you, son? He leaves me alone, knows I like me solitude. . . He's more like his mother in that respect.' The woman stared pensively into the flames of the fire and Olivia saw that Jake had followed her gaze. What was he thinking about? 'Ah, now she was a lady, a *real* lady. Suffered a lot in those last few years, but kept a brave face on everything. Shame she's gone. . .dreadful shame. . .'

'I think it's time we left.' Jake spoke suddenly, shaking himself out of his reverie. 'You'll be all right, Grace?'

The old woman nodded. 'Course I will!' She gave him a slow, considering look. 'More to the point, my lad, will you?'

'Don't start fussing about me, Grace, I'm fine.' Jake's voice was sharp, but it didn't seem to upset the old woman. He paused and when he spoke again his voice held less of an edge. 'We really must be going.'

'I know. I know you're a busy man.' She shook her head as Jake strode purposefully out of the sitting-room, grasping Olivia's arm as she got up to follow behind. 'Look after him,' she muttered. 'It's not going to be easy, but then, I can see from your face that you know that. Loving a man like Jake Savage. . .' The old woman shook her head sagely. 'You *do* love him, don't you?' Olivia nodded silently and she continued with satisfaction, 'Of course you do; it's written all over your face. *He* won't see it, though. Hurt by a woman and then the shock of the accident to deal with. He's still grieving and he's not letting any of it out. It's not good.' She shook her grey head again. 'Not good at all. He blames himself, see?'

Olivia frowned. 'For what?'

The room darkened suddenly as Jake appeared in the doorway. 'Are you coming? Or do you expect me to wait all day?'

Olivia flushed, conscious of his sharp gaze. She murmured her goodbyes to the old lady and then slowly followed Jake out to the Range Rover, dwelling on what the old woman had said.

'What was Grace talking to you about?'

His enquiry wasn't a casual one, Olivia sensed that immediately. 'Oh, just her cats,' she murmured, hating herself for lying, but feeling that there was no other choice. 'She. . .seemed to know a lot about your family,' she added quietly. 'She spoke about your mother with a great deal of affection—'

'She *thinks* she knows a lot,' Jake replied shortly. 'She's just an old woman who likes to gossip.'

Shutters down. Conversation closed. All enquiries to cease. Olivia glanced back at the dilapidated house and wished she had more information from Grace to help her.

'I can see you're glad that's over.'

'It was an. . .experience,' Olivia replied honestly.

'You're regretting your decision to come along, aren't you?'

'N. . .no—'

'Oh, come on! You don't have to pretend,' Jake delivered abruptly. 'You were like a cat on a hot tin roof the whole time we were there!'

'Was that an intended pun?' Olivia enquired frostily.

He looked at her without amusement. 'No,' he replied.

'No, of course it wasn't,' Olivia flashed. 'You don't have anything even remotely resembling a sense of humour, do you?'

'Don't start taking your frustrations out on me!'

'What frustrations?' Olivia demanded.

'You were like a fish out of water in that house just now and you didn't like it.'

'It was a little difficult for me at first, I'll admit that,' Olivia replied. 'It was a new experience.'

'Oh, and you're into acquiring those, are you?' His mouth curled without amusement.

'Why are you so angry?' Olivia turned towards him, her face ablaze. 'Because Grace dared to talk about your private life in front of me, is that it?'

'She said nothing of any importance!'

'Well, what, then?' she demanded, scanning the chiselled features for clues.

He glared down at her, his features taut. 'Damn it, have you forgotten why we came?' He shook his head and released a slow breath, dragging fingers through his thick, dark hair. 'An animal died!' he gritted after several seconds of tense silence. 'If she had only spotted the cat earlier,' he murmured flatly. 'I saw the patch of blood when I went out to bury it. The poor thing must have lain for some considerable time in the back garden only yards from the back door.'

Olivia frowned, cursing herself for still not knowing him. He cared, he really did. She could see it in the intensity of his expression. 'But you didn't tell Mrs Wood that?' she murmured.

'No, of course I didn't—what do you take me for?' Jake replied abruptly. 'She would have felt a hundred times worse than she already does.'

Olivia narrowed her eyes. She felt the beginnings of understanding. This man had so many hidden layers, each one locked beneath the controlled, ruthless persona, only to be revealed on the very rarest of occasions.

'Do you suffer this way every time an animal dies?' she asked quietly.

He hesitated and for a split-second Olivia thought she had made some kind of real breakthrough; there was a softening of the rugged features, a startled flicker of warmth in the ebony eyes, and then it was gone, dragged back behind the cold, metallic mask. 'No, of course not.' He moved away from her and walked over to his vehicle, parked on the side of the road. 'If I allowed myself to become personally involved I'd be finished within the week.'

'Are we still talking about your work here, or have we moved on to other areas of your life?' Olivia murmured.

He ignored her comment, opening the door of the Range Rover to throw his bag inside.

'It was a dreadful shame you weren't able to do something,' Olivia continued, following him, desperate to make contact again, to break through the defensive barrier that was an unfathomable part of their relationship. 'Although surely the old woman would have been in dreadful difficulties if the cat had lived?'

He turned to face her. Dark brows rose in cool query. 'Why's that?'

'The. . .the cost of trying to get such a badly damaged animal well again. . .' Olivia murmured. 'I know vet's fees are quite expensive and—'

The harsh mouth tightened. 'You think I would have *charged*?'

'Well. . .it's usual, isn't it?' she flared defensively, immediately realising her mistake. 'That's what vets do!'

'Not this one,' Jake replied sharply. 'At least not where old women, who only have their pension to live on, are involved—got it?'

'I don't know why you're attacking me like this!' Olivia flashed, hating him, hating the fact that he wasn't interested in giving her a chance. 'Is it my fault that poor cat went and got run over? Am I to blame because of that?'

'No, of course you're not! Don't be ridiculous!'

'Well, why are you taking it all out on me, then?' Olivia demanded. 'Why are you being so. . .so. . . hateful?'

'You hardly said two words.'

'I made her some tea. I got her a biscuit when she asked for one.'

'Big deal!'

Olivia felt her throat tighten. 'You're not being fair!' she gritted.

He threw her an icy look. 'No. I never am.'

'Who was the woman?' She hesitated a second. 'Grace said you were—'

'I know what she said!' He glanced across at her and

she saw the annoyance in his gaze. 'I've told you, Grace is an old gossip.'

'You're angry because she mentioned your family in front of me,' Olivia continued. 'Because she, of all people, dared to broach the big, taboo subject of your private life in my presence!'

'You don't need to know,' Jake responded tightly. 'It's over. Finished.'

'But can't you see?' Olivia continued. 'It's affecting our relationship.'

'Only because you seem to continually want to pry into something that's no concern of yours!' Jake flashed.

It was delivered like a blow. He certainly knew how to hurt, Olivia thought miserably. 'Forget the trip back to your place,' she replied stiffly. 'I can walk home from here.' She took a deep breath and tried to control her trembling voice. 'It's obvious my presence irritates you beyond endurance—!'

The car phone bleeped insistently, interruping her frustrated retort. Jake reached inside and lifted the receiver, saying little as usual, his face a mask of cool control once again. Olivia waited impatiently, knowing she should walk away, but finding curiosity getting the better of her as it became increasingly clear that Jake was needed elsewhere.

He looked across at her as the phone call came to an end. 'It's probably best if you don't come with me on this one.'

Olivia swallowed and took another steadying breath. 'Why?'

'There's a colt that has lacerated himself on a sharp fence post. . .' There was a pause. 'It's Sophie's horse.'

She didn't need time to decide. In a moment Olivia

was walking around the vehicle towards the passenger seat. 'I want to come,' she declared decisively.

Jake made no comment. He started the engine and manoeuvred the Range Rover out of the village without a word.

He saw to the beast outside in the paddock where it had injured itself. He injected the good-looking animal with a general anaesthetic and in no time the horse was lying out cold amongst the buttercups.

Sophie cradled her animal's head in silence, whilst Jake washed his hands in a bucket of water, dried them on a towel and then set about repairing the damage to the flesh.

Olivia had expected all sorts of irate reactions from Sophie at her presence. It had been a blessed relief to see an embarrassed half-smile on the younger girl's face when she'd arrived with Jake, even if it had been placed there for the sole benefit of her hero.

'A clean wound,' Jake commented as he threaded a needle with gut. 'Although pretty extensive.' He looked across at Sophie and smiled. 'No long-lasting damage. He should heal well.'

She was clearly relieved. Olivia watched intently from a discreet distance as Jake repaired the laceration between the two front legs with swift, neat stitches.

When he had finished, Olivia, feeling that she should contribute something, stepped forward and offered to clean the instruments that littered a steel tray at Jake's feet. He looked mildly surprised, but made no comment, simply bending down to retrieve the dish containing his implements and handed it over to her.

'Jake. . .could you come inside the house and wash your hands? I'd like to have a word with you.'

Olivia glanced up as Sophie spoke, and then lowered

her head to her task, crouching on the grass as she swilled the instruments in the clean bucket of water.

They wandered over to the large thatched cottage together, with Olivia resolutely refusing to watch them as they strolled side by side.

She finished her task swiftly and carried the clean, wet instruments and the bucket of dirty water over towards the Range Rover, which was parked next to the house.

She caught the sound of their voices as she tipped the used water down the drain. It wasn't difficult. The kitchen window was open because of the heat and neither of them seemed to make any effort to lower their voices. Olivia busied herself with opening the Range Rover's rear door and stowing the instruments inside. Then she bent to the outside tap and washed her hands, splashing the cool running water onto her face. It was very hot now and she didn't fancy sitting inside the baking vehicle until Jake emerged from the house.

She had honestly never intended to listen in to Jake's and Sophie's conversation, but the sound of her own name, spoken by Jake, made her halt momentarily.

'. . .you really mustn't feel threatened by Olivia,' he was saying reassuringly. 'Her presence has no connection with the way I feel about you.'

Olivia drew a breath and found that her feet were suddenly rooted to the spot. She listened deliberately with a despairing heart, sensing that what she was about to hear would not make her feel the slightest bit better.

'I know that. Yes, I do!' Sophie sounded earnest, contrite even. 'You're right, Jake. And I'm sorry I behaved so badly at the May ball; it's just that every time I see you—'

'I know.' Jake's voice was flat, almost weary. 'It's not as bad as it was, though, is it? You just need to give it time,' he added softly. 'You have to be patient. Things will work out.'

'Will they?' She didn't sound particularly convinced, Olivia thought. 'You won't ever desert me, will you, Jake?' she continued breathlessly. 'I just couldn't bear it if you forgot me—'

'No, sweetheart...' Olivia closed her eyes at the endearment '...of course I won't.'

It served her right for listening, of course. Olivia moved away and walked towards the paddock in a haze of misery.

'All finished?' Jake emerged from the house alone. 'Olivia!' She heard her name, but didn't turn to look at him. 'Where do you think you're going?'

He caught up with her and walked alongside for a pace or two. 'Olivia, didn't you hear me? I was talking to you.' He gave her a moment and when Olivia didn't reply he caught her arm and swung her around to face him. 'What's wrong?'

'Oh, nothing!' Olivia's eyes glistened. 'Just the usual—me getting all emotional again!'

'What on earth for? Sophie hasn't said anything to you—I've been with her all the time.' His voice was cool.

'Oh, no, it's not Sophie.' She sounded harsh, bitter with anguish.

Jake raised a dark brow and pierced Olivia with a look. 'Do you want a lift back to your place now?'

He knew how to hurt; a simple enquiry and a

dismissal all rolled into one. He had had enough. For now, or for good? Olivia wondered frantically.

'Could we get Mutt first?' she asked unsteadily. 'He's mended now and you said I could have him.'

'If that's what you want.' His voice was flat.

'Well, actually. . .' Olivia stopped walking. She stared down at her hands and saw that her fingers were shaking so much that she had to clench them into fists. 'Actually, it's not what I want, not at all!' she cried impulsively. 'You know that!'

She met his gaze for a second as he turned in surprise to stare at her and then she ran wildly across the paddock towards the gate that led out onto the lane.

Her legs were like jelly, her lungs were crying out for air when he reached her. Jake caught hold of her arms, spun her around to face him, and without a word crushed her trembling mouth with his own in a kiss that communicated all of the need and passion that they had both felt from the very beginning.

'My place,' he growled, releasing her at last.

'Jake. . . I don't think I can go on like this—!'

'My place. No arguments,' he repeated insistently.

And she succumbed under his formidable vitality, just as she always had done, just as she always would do.

They just about reached the mansion before they began removing each other's clothes. Jake slammed the heavy front door shut behind them and pulled Olivia close against his rugged frame, slipping her blouse over her head as he did so, kissing her neck, her throat, before carelessly ripping his own shirt from his body.

She heard the tearing of cloth and felt a warm glow of immense pleasure as the sound filled the silence of the house. He wanted her as badly as she wanted him. It would be all right; he would love her one day. He *would*.

He lifted her into his arms suddenly and carried her up the wide staircase, swinging her around once they reached the landing to push open a door.

His bedroom was vast, the room of a man who was rich and successful, who liked paintings and books and antiques. The bed was firm, a six-foot-square ocean of navy and maroon. Olivia fell amongst the waves and held out her arms to Jake, yearning for the intense pleasure his body could bring, praying desperately that she would be able to break down the barriers that existed between them.

Their lovemaking was urgent and frantic and utterly satisfying, every part of her responding fervently to his lean, strong body as he guided her towards the ultimate discovery, the ultimate sensation.

'You look replete.'

Olivia released a breath, twisting over on her side to face him. 'Do I?' She felt it. Despite everything. There was a dreadful emptiness deep inside, but she refused to allow it to come to the surface. It would only spoil the moment and she didn't want that.

Jake lifted a hand and threaded his fingers through her hair, lifting the blonde strands so that they glinted in the late-afternoon sunlight. 'You're very beautiful,' he murmured, 'like an angel.'

'No wings,' Olivia murmured, reaching out to touch the bronzed skin, 'and I shout too much.'

'This afternoon you've had good reason.' Jake leant forward and kissed her mouth gently. 'I can be pretty unreasonable on occasion.'

Olivia arched her eyebrows. 'Only on occasion?'

The firm mouth quirked into an attractive smile. 'Watch it, lady!' he murmured. His dark eyes sparkled with amusement as he traced the tip of his finger over her bare skin. 'Don't you know you're treading a very dangerous path?'

'I know.' Olivia gazed into the smouldering eyes with their fringe of spiky lashes and thought about how much she loved him. 'Believe me, I know,' she whispered.

He let out a breath. 'I have my reasons for behaving as I do, Olivia. It really is best this way.'

'Who for?'

There was a second's hesitation. 'I can't be the man you want me to be,' Jake told her quietly. 'It's important you understand that.' He trailed a path between the curves of her breasts. 'I am what I am.'

'A complex man. . .with a sadness in his life, who won't let anyone get close.'

Immediately she knew that she had said too much. The finger stilled; the handsome face regained some of its familiar rigidity.

'You think you know me?' His voice held a derisive edge. 'How clever you must be.' He moved away, breaking their contact suddenly, rolling towards the edge of the bed, holding his head in his hands. 'When I hardly feel I know myself at times.'

She wanted to comfort him, to reach out and touch the broad back, to cover his skin in a thousand kisses, to tell him how much she cared, but she knew he would rebuff any contact. 'Not clever,' Olivia replied quietly, thinking about destiny and their first meeting, wondering if fate was playing a huge, unfunny joke, 'just observant.'

'Well, if you're so observant then you must know that I'm compelled by you. Every time, every single time I lay eyes on you I want to make love to you. I'm compelled,' he repeated slowly, 'but that doesn't mean I *enjoy* feeling that way, does it? Compulsion.' He shook his head. 'Maybe it's a family trait; my father lived with it for years—so did my mother.' He cursed beneath his breath. 'I wish to God it weren't.'

'I don't understand.'

'I don't expect you to.' He glanced back at her. 'I don't *want* you to.'

'Sophie...' Olivia's voice quivered a little, but she forced herself to continue.'Does this have something to do with her?'

'Sophie?' He nodded slowly. 'In a way.'

'She loves you.'

'No, she doesn't.'

'Jake, she does! I've heard her speak. I've seen the way she looks at you.'

'You've seen nothing. You know nothing!' His voice was like a shaft of ice.

He rose from the bed and Olivia found her gaze drawn towards the solid muscles of his chest, the V-shaped haze of dark hair, not surprised any more by the swift ache of desire she felt inside. Her mouth quivered as she tried to blank out the misery his words had produced. She wouldn't let him see that it mattered; she couldn't.

Jake surveyed her rigidly, his ebony eyes scanning her feminine curves with an expression that conveyed that a battle was taking place within. 'How many times do I have to tell you? I'm not interested in any emotional involvement. I told you that in the beginning. I've told you that a hundred times since! It wouldn't work. I'm not the type.' He reached out, pulled on a pair of shorts and made to leave the room. 'There's a shower through there and some clean shirts in one of those drawers,' he informed her crisply. He paused, one large hand gripping the edge of the door, and looked back towards the rumpled bed. 'Olivia!' Dark brows drew together in a fierce scowl. 'Will you stop looking at me like that? Have I lied to you?' he insisted savagely. 'Have I cheated or deceived you? Have I led you to believe that things would be anything other than what they are? *Have* I?'

Olivia swallowed, feeling the helplessness, the inevitability of her answer. 'No.'

It was the answer he wanted, but it didn't seem to give him any satisfaction. The harsh mouth tightened and then Jake pulled the door closed behind him and left the room.

# CHAPTER EIGHT

JAKE was making tea in the kitchen. Olivia paused in the doorway, watching as he poured water from a steaming kettle into a cheerful pottery teapot. The scene of domesticity made her want to cry. She swallowed and took a hasty breath. Tears were not allowed.

'I think I'll walk Mutt home. Have you got a lead I can borrow?'

'There's one in the drawer.' He looked up, but only briefly, his eyes flicking swiftly over her slim frame, clad in one of his own baggy denim shirts.

There was a silence. Through an open window Olivia could smell newly cut grass, hear a blackbird singing loudly. She retrieved the lead from the drawer, gripping it tightly in her hands. Spring; a joyous, hopeful time. A time of new beginnings and fresh starts. . .

Olivia's eyes alighted on the photograph just as she was about to shut the drawer. It was an old passport photo of Jake, not a very good one, but then, they never were. Instinctively her fingers curled around its worn edges. Clearly it had been in the drawer some time; Jake's hairstyle was slightly different, a little longer, a little wavier. . .

'Do you want some tea before you go?'

She jumped as if caught stealing, but didn't let go of the photograph. She wanted it. She had to have it. When their relationship ended she would be able to look at this image and remember the times they had spent together. . .

'Olivia?' He was looking across at her.

She pushed the drawer shut, feeling the dryness of her mouth and her throat. She didn't want to leave him at all, that was the problem. You fool, she thought as she nodded in reply. Any excuse to stay a while longer, to be in the presence of this man. . .

Jake carried the mugs across to the large pine table that dominated the room. 'Your clothes are here.' He picked up a navy and white pile from a chair and placed it next to Olivia. 'Mutt's outside, if you're wondering,' he murmured, taking a mouthful of scalding tea. 'My housekeeper must have put him out in the garden when she left earlier. Do you want me to give you both a lift home? I can bring his basket—'

'No!' Olivia's harsh reply rang out awkwardly in the cavernous kitchen. 'No. I. . . I feel like some fresh air.' She met Jake's cool gaze over the rim of her mug. 'To clear my head,' she added miserably.

'As you like.' He looked uncaring, leaning back in his chair to place strong arms behind his head.

'And I don't need the basket,' Olivia continued determinedly. 'I want to buy one for myself.'

The firm mouth hardened slightly, increasing her unease. 'Suits me. I bring home the odd stray sometimes—it comes in useful.'

Olivia stood up. She couldn't take any more of this. 'I'm going!' she announced. 'I'll just change.' She began picking up her clothes.

'Do it here.' Jake rose from his chair and strolled over to the outside door. 'I'll go and find Mutt for you.'

Olivia pulled her shorts on swiftly, thrusting the photo of Jake carefully into one pocket. She felt so angry, so frustrated. The pretence, the forced coldness, the charade of making him believe she was coping with everything was draining in the extreme. Wasn't it madness to put herself through so much agony? Wouldn't the wisest thing be to admit defeat and give up now?

Jake returned, inevitably, with Mutt bounding at his heels, just as Olivia was about to pull her striped top over her head. No bra. No dignity. No pride. She blushed furiously as she struggled with the cotton and Lycra material, becoming more entangled and more embarrassed as the seconds passed.

His eyes strayed to her body, as she had known they would, the dark gaze lingering appreciatively over the curves that he had caressed so effectively less than an hour ago.

'Don't come near me!' Olivia cried as he crossed the room towards her. She stood clutching her top against her, exposed and vulnerable before him, acutely conscious of her naked breasts.

He met her gaze without comment for a moment, then reached forward and suddenly his strong capable fingers were touching her, moulding, fondling, scorching all her senses into life. Oh, how easily he could manipulate her! Olivia tried to stifle a gasp and failed miserably as his fingers continued their erotic massage. The surge of intense desire was spiralling into life all over again as his thumb caressed the dark brown nipple, as it became hard and erect, as the ache, deep down in the pit of her stomach, grew and intensified.

'Just like the first time we made love,' he murmured softly. 'You got yourself in a tangle then, do you remember?'

'I remember.' Mutt was bounding at their heels. The birds were singing, the sun was shining, and Jake had made it plain that he only wanted her body, only wanted this.

'Well?' His voice sounded husky now—clearly, touching her so intimately was affecting him as strongly as it was Olivia. She forced herself to look into his face, frowning slightly, as if the meaning of his question wasn't clear. 'I want things to continue,' he asserted roughly. 'Do you?'

She nodded just once, an infinitesimal movement of her head that indicated the strength of his power over her. Satisfaction gleamed in the jet eyes. He leaned forward and brushed his lips over the softness of her mouth. 'Good,' he murmured, releasing her.

Disappointment replaced desire. She had expected him to hold her close, had longed for him to touch her even more intimately. Olivia looked up into the arrogant face and saw that he knew it.

She placed the denim shirt on the table and called Mutt to her, clipping the lead to his collar.

Jake didn't come after her. Deep down it was what she had really expected. Olivia took a deep breath, shut the door behind her and set out for home with a heavy heart.

A week passed and Olivia's cottage became warm. No contact from Jake, but she refused to dwell on the implications of not hearing from him. Keeping busy, that was the key. Her shiny brand-new Jeep was delivered and she became mobile, buzzing around the village, breathing life into the venture that she was determined should succeed.

The decorators arrived, and the fresh smell of paint invaded the house. Pieces of furniture were sought out and installed with much care and thought. Another day, then another. More plans, more progress, but still no word from Jake.

Until. . .

Olivia picked the phone up breathlessly. She had been lugging a heavy pine chest to a new position and it had worn her out. 'Hello?'

The one time she picked up the receiver without thinking first that it might be him and it was.

'Are you in this evening?'

The sound of his voice, deep and masculine, made her gasp a little. She cleared her throat, hesitating, conscious of the terse edge to his voice. No preamble. No, Hello, how are you? I've missed you like crazy. Why was he angry? Where had he *been*?

'Yes, I'm in.'

'I want to speak to you. I'll be over at seven'

Nine days since she had last laid eyes on him. A lifetime trying not to think about him. Don't be such a doormat! a small voice cried angrily. He's walking all over you!

'It. . .it might not be convenient,' she murmured.

'Make it convenient!' he ordered. 'Seven. I'll be on time.'

Olivia stared at the phone. The decisive click that had terminated their brief conversation still echoed in her ear. To say he hadn't sounded particularly pleased would have been an understatement. She glanced at her wrist-watch. One hour before he arrived. One hour to get ready. She bit nervously down on her lower lip and tried not to imagine why he had sounded so angry.

Before long Olivia was checking her appearance in the mirror above the small hall table. She had carefully styled her hair so that the blonde tresses curled and shone, framing her carefully made-up face. She felt sick

with nerves. She straightened the rust cashmere
jumper, which matched her slim-fitting trousers exactly,
and took a steadying breath, before answering the
knock on the door.

He looked different. More rugged, more swarthy. A
growth of beard shadowed his jaw. Seeing him again
was wonderful. Olivia exhaled a shaky breath and
managed a smile. 'Hello.'

Dark eyes speared her face. He passed her by
without a word and walked into the living-room.

What had she expected? Immediate and overwhelming passion? An embrace, a word, a kiss that would
dispel all of her fears and her doubts?

'I hear you've been busy.'

Olivia turned to face him, eyeing his taut expression
warily. 'Yes.' She glanced deliberately around at the
room, her eyes resting briefly on the colourful rugs and
cushions and solid wooden furniture that gleamed with
polish and the patina of old age. 'As you can see, the
cottage is just about finished. And I've begun to make
arrangements for the tea garden too!' She moved
towards a tray of drinks and began pouring from a
decanter. 'I've ordered some tables and chairs and. . .
and I've found someone in the village who's willing to
bake for me; scones and fruit cake and—'

'That's not what I'm talking about and you know it!'

Olivia frowned, turning with a glass in each hand,
trying to maintain a look of puzzled innocence. 'Oh?'

'Come on, Olivia! You can do better than that! I'm
not stupid, and neither are you! Or, at least, that's what
I used to think. Maybe you are, because you don't
seem to understand a simple no when you hear it!'

'I. . .don't know what you're talking about.'

'Don't you?' Jake shot her a look. 'Are you going to

hand over that drink or not?' he demanded suddenly, moving towards her. 'God knows, I'm in need of it!' He removed the tumbler from Olivia's outstretched hand, tipping the amber liquid down his throat as if he were a man dying of thirst. 'I hear you've been rushing around the village in my absence, organising everyone left, right and centre!'

Olivia inhaled a little breath. He'd heard, then. 'Not rushing exactly.'

Ebony eyes glittered. 'Well, *what* exactly? Care to tell me?'

She turned back to the drinks tray, hating the look of savage anger on his face. 'I. . . I thought we could talk over dinner,' she murmured unsteadily. 'I've made the sauce. I just need to put some water on for the pasta.'

'Damn the pasta! I want to discuss it now. Or are you still trying to work out a way of telling me that *you've* decided to open up *my* house to the public as part of your damned village tour?'

'I. . . I haven't!' she stammered, turning back to face him. 'I just mentioned the idea to a few people, that's all.'

'Practically the whole of the village!' Jake thundered. 'I was accosted almost as soon as I arrived back—the vicar actually phoned me to say how pleased he was, how magnanimous it was of me to put up with all the crowds and the inconvenience—'

Olivia frowned. 'You've been away?'

'Yes.'

Her heart thudded. 'Where?'

'Germany, Belgium. . .' he shook his head as if it was unimportant '. . .Switzerland—'

'You've been to half of Europe and you didn't mention you were going!' Olivia cried.

He glared across at her. 'Why should I? Anyway, it was a spur-of-the-moment decision. A series of seminars. I'd been invited ages ago and decided not to bother, then changed my mind. It was just conferences,' he added as Olivia hung her head. 'Work. Boring as hell!'

'You could have mentioned you were going,' Olivia persisted. 'When you didn't contact me I thought. . . well, I thought things had changed between us.'

'Too right they've changed!' Jake growled angrily. 'You seem to have taken it upon yourself to interfere in my life. What the hell did you think you were *doing*?'

'I thought I was helping! I thought trying to raise money for a charity was supposed to be a good thing!' Olivia replied heatedly. 'I never expected this! I never expected you to come barging into my house, treating me as if I had commited some kind of criminal act!' She paused and gulped a series of ragged breaths, conscious of the tension in Jake Savage's frame. 'Is it so wrong,' she said shakily, 'to try to help?'

There was a long pause. Angry tension filled the air. Jake's eyes looked hard and unforgiving. Olivia thought of all the hours she had spent by the telephone, wondering when, if he was going to call. She loved this man and he didn't give a damn.

Jake lifted a hand and dragged it impatiently through his dark hair, cursing beneath his breath as he did so. 'Maybe I should have stayed in Europe,' he muttered wearily. 'Maybe it would have been better for everyone.'

'You really believe that?' Olivia's voice dropped to a whisper. The thought that there would probably come a time when she would never see Jake again reduced her anger to zero. Nine days had been long enough; a lifetime without this man was unthinkable. She held her breath, watching him, waiting for his dreaded reply.

'I can't say I haven't seriously given it some thought,' he informed her wearily. 'Particularly in the light of recent events.' Jake sent her an impatient look. 'A fresh start, the chance to begin again in a place where nobody knows or cares about your past or your present. You've done it. You escaped from your life in London. Maybe I should forget my responsibilities and do the same somewhere else.'

'Oh, that's right! Just walk away! Abandon everything!' She wanted to add, Abandon me, but managed to refrain from yelling such an obvious line.

'You really don't know when to stop, do you?' Jake demanded. 'You knew what my feelings were and yet you had the audacity to go on in spite of all I said.'

'I only mentioned the idea to a few people,' Olivia repeated fervently. 'I told you!' She released a long breath of disbelief. 'Look, I don't understand why you're being like this. It's for a good cause. I spoke to the vicar about the church-roof appeal and he was absolutely delighted that I wanted to help. Everything's going so well. The people of the village are rallying around; I held a meeting to see who'd like to be involved and there was lots of positive response. That very pretty cottage near the green, for instance. . .the couple are keen gardeners, and they're going to sell plants and—'

'I don't want to hear about your damned arrangements!' Jake thundered. 'Can't you understand that I'm just not interested?'

'Well, you should be.' Hurt rose to the surface. Olivia

glared across the room at him. 'You damned well should be! I've worked hard getting this together. I've been in contact with local printers and magazines—' she gulped a breath, watching as Jake glared at her in disbelief. 'What is so dreadful about opening up a couple of your rooms to the public? I'm only talking about one day a week,' she added, 'one measly day! You probably won't even be around, you'll be at your surgery, or out on calls. I don't know why you're being so unreasonable about this, so angry—'

'Is it because we're lovers?' he gritted. 'Do you think that because we've shared a bed it gives you some right to organise my life?'

Olivia stared, aghast. 'No!' she protested. 'No, of course not!'

'Well, what, then?'

'I just wanted to help,' Olivia replied miserably. 'That's all. I just wanted to show you—'

'Ah, now we're getting to the point,' Jake thundered. 'You couldn't take no for an answer, could you? You felt an overwhelming urge to try to prove some sort of point.'

'No.' Olivia shook her head. 'It's not like that. I just want to do something worthwhile. Why are you so angry? Many of the villagers told me how good your family were about this sort of thing—'

'Ah, yes! My family.' Jake's expression was suddenly inexplicably amused. 'Absolute paragons of the charitable event.' There was a short, harsh laugh. 'Even my dear, departed father secretly insisted on doing his bit around the village. Of course, my mother didn't find out until quite some time later—'

'Look, I don't know what you're talking about, but I'm sick of this,' Olivia cried. 'You're twisting my motives to suit yourself. I wanted to help. Is there something so wrong in that? I wanted to show that I was willing to be a useful, caring part of the community. It may seem ridiculous to you, but it's been my lifelong dream to live in the country, to own a house like this with a thatched roof and pretty little windows. I wanted to be happy and content and. . .and peaceful. Then I met you!' Olivia took a shuddering breath and listened to the beating of her heart. 'We may be lovers,' she added shakily when Jake made no reply. 'but it means nothing to you, does it? Absolutely nothing!'

'That's not true.'

His voice, low and vibrant, stopped Olivia in her tracks. She looked across at him. After her violent outburst the room seemed strangely quiet. '*What*?'

'Of course what we have together means something!' Jake gritted, flashing her a fierce look. 'What do you take me for, some kind of automaton?'

'You. . .you act as if you have no feelings,' Olivia replied, looking totally drained.

'I *act* a great deal, full stop.' He murmured in reply. 'For the past three years I feel as if I've done nothing except play a part.'

Olivia shook her head. 'I don't understand,' she told him flatly. 'Not at all.'

'The responsible elder brother. The tragic lord of the manor!' There was a tense silence. 'I missed not being with you whilst I was away,' Jake delivered quietly, keeping his eyes fixed on her face. 'I didn't expect that.'

Olivia hesitated. She wanted to run to him and throw her arms around his neck, but she managed to restrain herself somehow. 'I see.'

He looked fierce again. 'Is that all you can say?'

She shot him a glance. 'What do you want me to say?'

Another tense silence. For one heart-stopping moment Olivia thought that he was going to actually tell her, but the hope died as soon as he opened his mouth and she was immediately glad she had held on to some dignity. 'OK. You said one day a week. Make it Thursday,' he instructed roughly. 'I'll get my house-keeper to take the shrouds off the downstairs rooms. Charge whatever you like. But there's one condition.'

The shock was so great that Olivia could hardly speak. 'Wh. . .what's that?'

'You're responsible. No one else. Just you.' He narrowed his gaze. 'Is that clear?'

She nodded slowly, and he turned on seeing her agreement and began heading towards the door.

'Jake!'

'Yes?'

There was a sick, sinking feeling inside. She had won this battle but it didn't mean a thing if he was going to turn away and walk out on her. 'You're. . .going?'

He slanted her a cool glance. 'It looks like it, doesn't it?'

'For. . .good?'

He released a taut breath. 'Maybe. Who knows?' He dragged a hand through his hair again. 'Look, I'm tired, Olivia. I've been to three countries in five days. I stepped off the plane and then had to attend an emergency at a farm as soon as I entered the village. I've got to get some sleep.'

'You could sleep here. The pasta will wait.'

He looked back at her, studying her pale face for a long while, and then the harsh lips curved momentarily into a smile. 'I hope not—I hate pasta.'

'Cornflakes. . .' Olivia hesitated a fraction, knowing she couldn't let him go '. . .in the morning—tea, toast, bacon and eggs. . .anything you like.'

'You're trying very hard to tempt me.'

'But am I succeeding?' She walked slowly towards him and every step felt like a mile. 'I just don't want us to fight,' she murmured, looking up at the taut, dark features. 'I don't want you to hate me, that's all.'

Strain clenched his dark features. She sensed the control he was having to exert. When he finally spoke it was as if the words had been dragged out of him. 'I don't. . . I don't hate you, Olivia.'

'Show me, then.'

He raised a hand and touched her cheek. 'You're an irresistible woman, do you know that?'

Olivia released a breath and smiled, conscious of the familiar desire that was growing between them. 'Do you have some clean clothes?'

Jake rubbed a hand along his unshaven jaw and looked puzzled. 'My case is still in the car, but I doubt there's very much in the way of clean laundry.' He frowned. 'What's that got to do with anything?'

Olivia smiled. He had been so fierce, and now he looked almost vulnerable, half asleep on his feet, too tired to think properly. 'Why don't you go upstairs and have a bath?' she murmured. 'There's lots of hot water. You look so tired—you can't drive home like this.'

'It's only a couple of miles up the road,' Jake pointed out, trying hard to stifle a yawn. 'I'm capable of making that sort of distance without falling asleep at the wheel.'

She stood on tiptoe and kissed his mouth softly. 'Upstairs!' she repeated quietly. 'Can't you recognise an order when it's given to you?'

'*You* are ordering *me*?' He stroked strong fingers

through the blonde waves around her face. Then
slowly, miraculously, he smiled and all the tension left
his body. 'I was angry with you.' His voice was unbe-
lievably tender and Olivia basked in the glory of it. 'I
intended to be angry with you for a long time. How
come I'm not any more?'

'I. . .don't know.' Olivia's eyes closed as he kissed
her lips. Nine days without him. It had felt like a
lifetime. 'Maybe you should go upstairs and have that
bath like I suggested and think about it,' she murmured. 'What do you say?'

'Will you promise to forget the pasta?'

Olivia opened her eyes and met the stunning ebony
gaze. 'Consider it done,' she smiled. 'Your wish is my
command.'


She couldn't remember the last time she had felt so
happy. Olivia hummed contentedly as she put a joint
of meat into the oven and set about laying the small
round table that nestled snugly in the corner of the
kitchen next to the cream Aga stove.

She was determined that tonight would be perfect.
She wouldn't allow anything to spoil it. Once Jake had
finished his bath, they would eat and drink wine and
then make love in front of the fire. They would talk
and laugh and he would see, she would *make* him see,
just how good their relationship really was, how wonderful it could be. . .

'He's here, isn't he?'

Mutt, who had been sleeping in the corner of the
room, barked violently and Olivia spun around, dropping the plate she was holding with a clatter. She stared
in astonishment at a wild-looking Sophie, who was

framed dramatically in the kitchen doorway as china fragmented at her feet.

'What on earth do you think you are doing—?' Olivia began, rooted to the spot by this sudden apparition. 'How did you get in?'

'The door was open.' Sophie stepped over the threshold into the kitchen. 'Don't bother to pretend Jake isn't here, because I saw his Range Rover on my way in. Just get him for me, will you?' she ordered 'I need him. It's urgent!'

'Now just you look here!' Olivia replied angrily, curling her nose up at the smell of alcohol on Sophie's breath. 'This is not on. You do not come barging into my home, demanding—'

Sophie's gaze swivelled to the table. 'I see you were planning a cosy meal—how nice!' Her eyes narrowed to slits. 'I guess he hasn't told you about our trip, then?'

Olivia frowned. She felt dread, cold and hard, creeping into her heart. 'What trip?'

'Ah, he hasn't!' Green eyes flashed their dislike. 'He did say it would be best if we kept it quiet—'

'I don't know what you're talking about,' Olivia responded coolly, urging a playful Mutt back into his basket, 'and I don't care. Now would you please just leave—'

'*Sophie*?' Jake had walked into the kitchen. Olivia glanced at the magnificent torso, at the towel slung low over his hips, and then looked away. She could hear the concern in his voice, see the evening disintegrating before her very eyes as he crossed the room and put his arm around the younger girl's shoulders. 'What are you doing here?'

'It's Saracen; there's something the matter with him. I tried to tell Olivia it was urgent, but she wasn't interested.' Sophie's voice had altered dramatically. 'Oh, Jake! Please come!'

Dark brows drew together. 'What's wrong exactly?'

'Well. . .he's off his food,' Sophie hesitated, 'and he's been rolling around and now he's just lying still. He's not interested in anything or anyone. Oh, Jake!' She put her arms around his waist and pressed her face against his bare chest. 'Please come; I'm so worried.'

'I don't believe this!' Olivia's voice rang out cold and heartless in the cosy kitchen.

'Tony can see to him for you. He's on call tonight. You know what a good vet he is,' Jake murmured.

The attractive face crumpled with concern. 'But I want you! Saracen knows you. Tony just doesn't care about him the same way you do.'

Jake released a controlled breath. 'Sophie, that's not true—'

'Jake, don't do this to me!' she cut in. 'You know how much that horse means to me.' She hung her head and began to cry quite pitifully. 'If I lose him, after everything that's happened, I just know I won't be able to cope. He's the only thing I've got left—apart from you, that is!'

'Hey! Shh. Calm down now.' Jake hugged the slender shoulders carefully. 'That's not going to happen.' He released a weary breath, glancing across at Olivia's rigid face and in that moment Olivia knew that she had lost and Sophie had won. 'OK, I'll go and get dressed. Sophie, go and wait outside in the car for me. I won't be more than a couple of minutes.'

'You're not really going?'

'Olivia, please,' Jake replied, once Sophie had left the room and was safely out of earshot. 'Don't start being difficult.'

'*Me*?' She glared at him in astonishment. 'What about precious Sophie? What's she being?'

'I won't be long. I'll take a look at her horse, put her mind at rest and then drive back. OK? We can still have this evening together.' He put his arms around Olivia's waist and kissed her neck. 'Will the food keep?' he murmured as Olivia, struggling to conceal the desire his touch produced, busied herself with turning various dials on the Aga, trying not to think of the evening she had hoped they'd have together. 'More importantly, will you?' he added softly.

'You'd better be going Jake. Sophie will be getting impatient,' Olivia murmured jerkily. 'After all, it wouldn't do to keep her waiting, would it?' she added, with more than a trace of bitterness.

She felt his strong arms fall from her waist and immediately regretted her retort. She hadn't meant her voice to come out sounding quite so awful. 'Jake—'

'If you're going to continue your impressive impersonation of a clinging woman then forget it!' he snapped. 'Believe me, this is the last thing I wanted to happen. But you could see how Sophie was—she's been drinking again and I've got to deal with it.'

'Why you? Why do *you* have to dash off into the night with Sophie?'

'I am not running off into the night!' Jake replied sharply. 'She's upset. She needs me.'

'*I* need you, dammit!' Olivia kept her face averted from his and walked over to the dining table in the corner of the room, deliberately scooping the cutlery onto the floor with a noisy clatter. She wanted to scream and shout with the unfairness of it all. Nine days apart and now Jake was leaving again—leaving to go to Sophie.

'I had no idea you could be so childish.' His tone held a daunting amount of cool detachment.

'I am *not* being childish!' Olivia snapped, spinning around. 'What's the point? It wouldn't get *me* anywhere, would it? Sophie maybe—it seems she can act anyway she wants! All *she* has to do is crook her little finger and you go running!'

'I don't want to explain,' he growled. 'Not now, not like this. Things are complicated. My relationship with Sophie is complicated.'

'Oh, I know it is.' Olivia stared at the demolished place settings in front of her and willed herself to stay strong for a few more moments yet. She picked up the two wine glasses from the table, gripping their stems tightly. 'Sophie's explained the situation only too clearly!'

'She has?' Jake sounded surprised. Olivia glanced across and saw that he looked surprised too. 'Well, in that case, you should know why I feel I have to go now.' He crossed the room and spun her towards him, glaring down into her rigid face. 'Do you think I *want* to leave?' he demanded roughly. 'Do you?' he repeated, jerking her closer so that the glasses slipped from her hands and smashed spectacularly on the tiled floor to join the broken plate and cutlery at her feet.

'You're going, aren't you?' Olivia croaked, still half hoping he would change his mind, watching the curt nod, feeling rejected all over again. 'Well, just go! Just go!' she repeated, pushing pointlessly against the strong, broad chest. 'Sophie's waiting for you!'

# CHAPTER NINE

THE evening stretched into night and Jake didn't return. He wasn't *ever* going to return. Olivia tortured herself with that thought, with the certainty of that knowledge, all through the interminable hours that followed his departure. She tortured herself with visions too. Jake and Sophie. Sophie and Jake. If she was a ship passing in the night, then Sophie was the harbour, a familiar haven where Jake would finally moor his vessel for good.

He cared for Sophie. There had been no mistaking the look of concern in Jake's expression when she had clung to him in the kitchen. He cared for her! But he doesn't care for me. All I've ever seen is lust, Olivia thought miserably. Anger and lust—it wasn't a particularly harmonious combination, and definitely not one that would stand the test of time, or one that should have hopes pinned on it, especially hopes that included love and marriage and the seductive image of her one day bearing Jake's child.

Olivia closed her eyes and drifted into an uneasy sleep, curling up in the corner of the settee, continuing the agony with visions of dreams that would never come true.

A sharp bang on the front door woke her well after midnight. She jumped violently, clutching a cushion, disorientated for a moment, waiting nervously until she heard the familiar voice calling her from outside.

Could she cope with seeing him again? No. But that

certain knowledge didn't seem to make any difference. She walked towards the door and drew back the bolts.

'I'm sorry it's late.' The dark, stunning eyes travelled over her rumpled clothing, lingering on the stifled yawn. 'I wasn't sure whether you'd be in bed, but as I drove past I saw the light. You needn't have waited up.'

'I didn't.' Olivia smoothed down her hair and tried to look as if she knew where she was. 'I was watching an old film. I'd been looking forward to it for ages.' A pointless lie—why had she bothered to say it? She saw straight away that he didn't believe a word of it. 'I. . . I didn't think you were going to return at all.'

Dark eyes glinted on her face. 'For a while I wasn't sure that I should.'

She steadied her breathing and walked back into the living-room. 'It's very late.' Olivia picked up some cushions from the settee and began to bash them into shape. 'And I'm extremely tired.'

'*You're* tired?' His tone was heavy. She glanced across and watched as he dragged strong fingers through his hair in a totally exhausted gesture. 'This evening has been an absolute nightmare. Sophie—'

'I don't want to know,' Olivia gritted, squeezing the cushions between her fingers. 'I don't need you to tell me that she had another one of her emotional tantrums!' She glared across at him, forcing herself to harden her heart. 'That's why you're so late, isn't it? Never mind the horse—Sophie was the one who ended up having to have all your attention! How was the beast, by the way?' she enquired sarcastically. 'At death's door?'

'Fine,' Jake replied sharply, 'Not a thing wrong.'

Olivia's eyes stung. 'You *knew*, didn't you?' she

flared. 'That it was a wild-goose chase, and yet you still trailed all the way over there! Why?' she demanded angrily. 'Why do you allow her to manipulate you so effectively?'

'She does not manipulate me!'

'No?' Olivia shook her head. 'Well, she gives a pretty good imitiation of it, then!'

Jake released a weary breath. He looked exhausted and Olivia had to harden her heart not to be affected by the sight of his drained expression. 'Olivia, I can do without this right now—!'

'I don't know why you bothered to come back.' She finished straightening the cushions and glanced around the room, avoiding Jake's glittering gaze, all the while hating herself for being so horrible. 'I don't suppose Sophie was particularly pleased, was she? What did you say to *her* when you left? That *Mutt* needed seeing to? He's asleep in the kitchen if you want to make a cursory examination,' she added tightly, gesturing towards the door in the far corner of the room. 'Go on! Go right ahead! I'm sure it will salve your conscience a little!'

'How long do you propose to keep this up?' The rough, angry note in his voice compelled her to look across at him. 'These snide, unhelpful remarks aren't getting either of us anywhere, are they? You know why I came back,' he thundered. 'You know you wanted me to come back. Don't play these pathetic cat-and-mouse games with me! I've experienced them before and I don't find them particularly attractive.'

'From Sophie, do you mean?' Olivia snapped. 'I should imagine she's a real whizz at tying people up in knots! One minute the helpless victim, the next—'

'Not Sophie, no!' Olivia gulped as Jake's rough

voice cut through her words. 'Will you give her a break?' he demanded. 'She's been through enough without you giving her a hard time!'

'Who, then?' Olivia risked a glance at the thunderous expression. 'If not Sophie, then who?'

'Never mind!' Jake gritted. 'Suffice to say that I learned several very useful lessons and in double-quick time!'

'Such as?' Olivia kept her eyes on him, aware of the bitterness in his tone.

The angular jaw tightened perceptively. 'That trust is not something you should give away too easily,' he shot back. 'That women, however beautiful, can be devious as hell. That the vast majority are attracted by wealth and power and influence—'

'One solitary female made you feel this way?' Olivia cut in disbelievingly. 'You got hurt and you condemn all women because of it?'

'Not all women, no.'

'No, of course not!' Olivia spun away and felt the ache in her heart. Just me, she thought, just me. 'Sophie couldn't possibly give you any grief.'

'Are you being dense on purpose?' Jake prowled around the sofa towards her. 'Look, I can see you're tired and disappointed that our evening was spoilt,' he said softly, 'but I'm here now—'

'You think. . .' Olivia gulped a breath, and worked hard at steadying her voice as he approached. 'You think that I would. . .allow you to. . .to. . .?'

'To what?' The ebony eyes were like chips of pure granite. 'Go on, Olivia,' he taunted. 'Finish the sentence. Remind me why I'm here, why I'm bothering to put up with all this ridiculous female hysteria.'

'I hate you!' she cried. He didn't care. It was obvious.

She loved him with a desperation that made her want to weep and he didn't give a damn, didn't have a clue. 'I hate you! You took her with you to Germany and Switzerland. . .and—'

'Belgium,' he finished.

'—and Belgium!' She took a step forward and threw the word in his face. 'Sophie took great pleasure in telling me that before you put in an appearance. I thought at first it was a lie, I *prayed* that it was a lie, but it's true, isn't it? *Isn't* it?' she persisted shakily when Jake didn't immediately reply.

'Yes.' His expression was grim. 'She pleaded with me to take her—'

Olivia closed her eyes momentarily, because her one last hope at being wrong had just died. 'I don't want to know.' Her voice rose an octave, cutting through Jake's rugged tones. 'I don't want to hear all the sordid details. Just work, you said, just seminars and conferences, and all the time the two of you were—'

'You think I *slept* with her?' The sheer force of his rage was shattering. Olivia gulped a breath and turned from him, but one large hand gripped her chin, giving her no other option but to meet his gaze. 'Don't you dare look away,' he commanded. 'You honestly believe I slept with Sophie?' He shook his head in disbelief. 'What sort of man do you take me for?'

'Don't insult me further by trying to deny it!' Olivia snapped, glaring up at him. He was a good actor, she thought miserably; his look of hurt outrage was almost convincing. 'I'm not a fool! I may have *acted* like a fool for the past two weeks, but I'm coming to my senses now! It was all talk in the beginning, about how you didn't want to make promises you couldn't keep, wasn't it?' she demanded tempestuously. 'About how you wouldn't deceive or lie. And my God!' Olivia's voice trembled, her eyes glistened, as she shook her head in amazement. 'I actually fell for it!'

'You are something else, do you know that?' Jake thundered. 'You saw what Sophie was like this evening. You know she's having problems. What was I supposed to do? Just tell her to go away?'

'I don't want to talk about her!' Olivia cried. 'You've used me and you think you can just waltz back in here and continue using me! Sex! It's all about sex—'

'Stop raising your voice.' Jake gripped her by the shoulders. 'You've said enough!'

'I'll raise my voice if I want to!' she flared. 'This is *my* house... I can behave how I please. I hate you! Do you hear me?' she yelled, beside herself now with misery and anger. 'I want you to know that. I want you to know how much I really hate you—!'

He wasn't listening any more. Large hands had snaked out towards her. Strong fingers curled around her upper arms and she was being dragged uncompromisingly towards the towering, solid frame. 'You think that matters to me now?' he roared at her. 'You honestly think that someone who could make love to a mixed-up girl like Sophie and then come back to you would *care*?' His hands tugged her closer and Olivia felt the bruising force of his mouth on her lips, the rough, searching anger of his touch. 'Only you,' he gritted savagely, 'only you make me act this way!'

She should have been fighting him off; if she hated him the way she said she did then she should have been screaming rape. But refusing his advances, however punishing they were, never entered her head. As Jake's hands roamed her body, as his mouth scorched her skin, she found herself becoming more and more aroused. They kissed as though they were enemies, but nothing, it seemed, could dispel the passion between them.

*Nine days*, Olivia thought as Jake lifted her into his arms and carried her towards the dying embers of the fire. Nine whole days. . .

He pinned her to the rug and covered her mouth with possessive hunger, as if he too was remembering how long it had been since they'd made love. Soon her lips were parting eagerly and merciless hands were grazing a path beneath the soft wool of her jumper.

'Strip!' The husky order sent shivers of desire down Olivia's spine. She stared up into Jake's rugged face, drinking in the forceful magnetism of his gaze, her breasts rising and falling with the effort of breathing.

'Jake—!'

'Strip!' he repeated. 'Do it!'

She hesitated, and then slowly, with fingers that trembled, Olivia began to remove her clothes, conscious of the dangerous power of the man, as he knelt above her, of the glittering ebony eyes that studied her every move.

After a time he reached out and pulled the lace ties at the front of her undergarment so that the coffee-coloured silk fell apart to reveal the full curves of her breasts and the smooth, flat planes of her stomach. His thumb traced a lazy path over her skin and Olivia watched as his hands set to work, gasping and moaning aloud as he ruthlessly teased and played with her. The firelight flickered over her skin and she saw the shadow of their bodies on the wall. She ached with wanting him, ached so badly that it was like a pain, low and deep in the pit of her stomach. . .

'Now take it off.'

Trembling, Olivia slipped the garment from her shoulders, wriggled it over her hips. She was held captive by his potent gaze. She sat up, mesmerised by the magnificent body in front of her, by the look on Jake's face that made her believe in that moment that she was the only woman in the world he wanted— would ever want.

His hands fell to the buttons of his shirt, then to the waistband of his trousers. She felt the intensity in his whole being and knew that his need was as urgent as her own. It didn't take him long to remove his own clothes. All the while he studied her, devouring every inch of her with molten eyes.

When they were both naked he seized her by the shoulders and pulled her to him, positioning her, moulding her, touching every part of her, so that soon Olivia was gasping aloud, begging him to continue what he had so furiously started.

He wasn't gentle. Each possessive thrust told her his anger was still strong, but it didn't matter. Whilst they made love he was a part of her, and she could blot out all of reality and concentrate on loving him, on pretending that he loved her too. . .

'You are the only woman who makes me feel this way.' It was a harsh admission, uttered just before they both reached the ultimate sensation, heavy with meaning and truth. But what meaning? What truth? The only woman that made him feel both angry and lustful?

A powerful combination, but not the right one.

Olivia closed her eyes and pressed her face against Jake's shoulder, gasping aloud as his final thrust took her over the edge and the stars shattered high above in their heavens. She held him close, gripping him to her, feeling the strength of his sweat-slicked body beneath her fingers.

I love you! she cried silently. I love you!

And in her dreams he said it too.

The room was deliciously warm, the bed fresh and clean, with crisp white linen sheets. Olivia slid beneath the cover and felt Jake climb in beside her.

He lay on his back and released a long-drawn-out breath, staring up at the recently painted ceiling for a long while in silence.

What was he thinking about? Olivia lay rigid, listening to the wind howling outside in the trees, hugging the quilt close to her naked body. Not Sophie, she thought desperately. Please don't let it be Sophie.

After several interminable minutes Olivia found the courage to speak, forcing the words out between trembling lips. 'Jake, I... I know you don't want to talk,' she murmured hesitatingly. 'But I have to know about Sophie. Are you going to marry her one day?' A sob rose in her throat and locked tight. She sniffed miserably. 'Jake? Did. . .did you hear what I said? I have to know. I have to know if our relationship means anything to you. . .anything at all.'

Silence.

Olivia opened her eyes and tilted her head towards the handsome profile. 'Jake?'

He was asleep. Deep, even breathing, the magnificent broad chest rising rhythmically in the half-darkness.

Cold dismay lurched into her stomach. He *was* made of stone. Surely this was evidence enough of how much she meant to him?

Olivia slid her body over to the cold edge of the bed,

pressed her face into the pillow and cried as if her heart would break.

She awoke late next morning to find Jake's strong body curved protectively around her own. His arm lay along the length of her thigh, the fingers of his other hand curved possessively around the fullness of her breast.

Despite her misery of the previous night, she knew it was a moment she would never forget; lying in the warmth of the bed, feeling him so close to her, smelling the seductive scent of his skin, dreaming that she was his and he was hers and that nobody would ever be able to take him from her.

He stirred a little in his sleep and Olivia automatically stiffened. She lay rigid, listening to the cheerful chorus of birds for a moment, and then tentatively she tried to move.

'Don't get up. Not yet.' His voice was husky against her ear, deeply masculine. Just hearing it made Olivia shiver with wanting him. 'This feels good,' he murmured sleepily. 'You may or may not believe it, but waking up on a sunny spring morning with a beautiful naked woman in my arms is not a usual occurrence for me.' He lazily stroked the length of her leg. 'You feel wonderfully warm and soft. Or rather you did,' he added, brushing his lips against her neck, 'until a moment ago. Don't go rigid on me, Olivia; it's early yet.'

She raised large blue eyes towards the carriage clock beside the bed. 'Actually it's late,' she murmured; 'almost ten.'

Jake kissed her neck again, tugging her close against his hard, muscular frame, so that his body curved around hers, so that she could feel every square inch of his solid male flesh. 'So, what does it matter? I haven't got anything to get up for, have you?'

'Did. . .did you sleep well?'

'Like a log.' His hands were exploring the length of her body; very slowly his fingers caressed the smooth contours of her thighs. 'What about you?'

'I woke up a couple of times,' Olivia admitted, hardly aware of what she was saying, so great was the distraction of Jake's touch. 'I. . . I couldn't quite believe you were still with me.'

His hand stilled. 'You thought I might have returned to Sophie?'

'I'll get us some tea.' Olivia, conscious of the hardness in Jake's tone, tried to twist away, but his hold was suddenly firm around her waist. 'Jake, please, it doesn't matter. I don't want us to argue—'

'Who said anything about arguing?' He gripped her shoulder and twisted Olivia around towards him. 'You really believe that Sophie and I. . .that she means something special to me, don't you?' he demanded. 'Hasn't last night gone any way to convincing you otherwise?'

Olivia scanned the hard expression nervously. 'You left me to go to her,' she pointed out quietly.

'And I came back to you,' Jake replied evenly. 'Doesn't that tell you anything?'

'I. . . I really don't want to talk about it.' Olivia glanced towards the window. He *had* come back, but there had only been one reason for his return, they both knew that. 'Look, it's a beautiful morning; let me get us breakfast.' She forced her voice to sound bright and cheerful. 'We can eat it in bed. I can't remember the last time I had breakfast in bed and I did promise you—Oh!'

'Forget breakfast. Forget everything except this!' Jake rose above her, pinning Olivia's arms to the pillow on either side of her head with one large hand. He brushed back her hair with the other and then took possession of her mouth in a gloriously fierce kiss that made her want him so swiftly, so intensely, that Olivia would have gasped aloud if she had been able. The hard masculine length of his body moved over her, pressing sensuously against her warm softness, inciting her quickly into a response that aroused them both, so that soon nothing mattered except touching and kissing and being together like this.

It got better every time. Olivia writhed impatiently beneath Jake's searching hands, desperate for the feel of him inside her. But as always he was in control, and as ever he made her wait, prolonging her impatient desires until she was mindless with wanting him, calling his name aloud, begging him to thrust her over the edge into the realms of glorious ecstasy.

They lay still in each other's arms for a long time afterwards. Not speaking, not wanting to spoil the moment. Each with their own private thoughts.

Finally Jake spoke. 'You've got to trust me,' he murmured. 'Our relationship isn't going to work if you don't.'

Olivia swallowed. 'We do have a relationship, then?'

He gave a short laugh. She felt his chest rise with it. 'Of course we do—what do you think we've just been doing?'

'Jake. . .' Olivia hesitated a fraction. 'Do you remember when we first met?'

'Of course.' He sounded amused. 'How could I forget?'

'Well, how did you feel. . .when you saw me?'

'Annoyed.'

Olivia's heart thudded. She remembered how she had felt in that first moment, so warm and excited, so full of knowing. Seeing Jake had been like coming home. He had been the one, the man she hadn't even realised she had been searching for all of her life. She steadied her breathing and tried to make her voice sound normal. 'I see.'

'No, you don't. No more do I. All I know is you appeared out of the blue and I wanted you the instant I set eyes on you.'

'But. . .but why should you feel annoyed about that?' Olivia queried unsteadily.

'I suppose because I've been working for so long to get my life on to some sort of even keel after the. . . accident.' There was an infinitesimal pause and Olivia knew he was thrusting away the pain of his parents' death. 'Seeing you, wanting to take you to bed so badly, I knew somehow you'd succeed in turning my life into one big complication.'

'I'm a *complication*?' Automatically her fingers gripped the quilted counterpane. 'That's how you look upon me?'

'Don't start getting uptight, Olivia.' Jake's voice held a warning note. 'You asked the question; I'm just trying to be honest.'

'Maybe I'd prefer it if you lied.'

'No, you wouldn't.' Jake's voice was steel-edged with certainty. 'If you were the sort of person who'd prefer lies then I wouldn't want to be with you. All relationships fester if they're based on lies.'

'Is that why you were so brutally honest with me in the beginning,' Olivia murmured, 'about our relationship?'

'It seemed like a good idea at the time,' Jake replied coolly. 'I wanted you to be under no illusion about how things would have to be if you became. . .involved with me.'

'And now?' Olivia whispered. 'Nothing's. . . changed?'

'Haven't I made it obvious enough that I still want you?' Jake delivered firmly. 'I told you how it was in the beginning, how things had to be between us, and I know it's been difficult for you to accept, but believe me, it's the best way—the only way. Emotional entanglements just don't interest me.'

'Isn't what you have with Sophie just that?' Olivia pointed out quietly.

There was a long silence. For half a moment Olivia thought Jake hadn't heard what she'd said. Then he spoke. 'When my family were killed we grieved together. Despite what you may think of her, she's a good person. She's finding things difficult at the moment, but—'

'She's *making* things difficult,' Olivia said under her breath. 'Are you sure you've been entirely straight with her?' she asked aloud.

'What are you talking about?' Jake's voice was terse. 'You seem continually determined to bring any conversation we have around to Sophie!' He slipped his arm away from Olivia and sat up in the bed, punching a pillow into shape as he did so. 'You're becoming obsessed with the girl!'

'Me? Obsessed?' Olivia shook her head a little in disbelief. She took a steadying breath and tried to keep her voice even. 'So have you been as brutally honest with her as you have been with me?' she persisted stonily. 'Does Sophie really know where she stands? Because, from what I've seen so far, I'd say—'

'From what you've seen!' Jake's eyes glittered. 'Olivia—' he took a breath, and as Olivia watched his hardened expression she saw that he was struggling to keep his temper '—I told you in the beginning that probing into my life, asking questions was out of bounds,' he stated coolly. 'It still is. Do you understand?' Olivia felt her lip trembling under the force of his gaze and hung her head, but he reached out and tilted her chin, so that she was forced to look back into his face. 'Do you?'

She nodded.

'And are you still willing to abide by those conditions? Because if you're not. . .' Jake left the sentence unfinished, but Olivia was in no doubt what the conclusion would be if she tried to object.

She felt utterly powerless. He was such a strong personality, so determined not to allow her to come close. Why? Did he really imagine that she only wanted him for his influence and wealth? Was that what he was so afraid of? But Jake Savage, afraid? Wasn't that a contradiction in terms?

'Olivia.' His voice was painfully intense. Olivia looked through the mist of tears and met the smouldering dark eyes. She loved him so desperately. Would revealing that fact change anything? she wondered. 'Can't you understand that when I'm with you I want to forget about the past?' he told her urgently. 'Don't start upsetting yourself with imagined fears. I told you in the beginning, I'm not interesting in playing around, in deceiving people. I didn't lie then and I haven't lied since.' He released a taut breath. 'We make love and the world feels a better place—isn't that enough?'

# CHAPTER TEN

'I'LL get us some breakfast.' Olivia slipped out of the bed and grabbed a towelling robe that was draped over the back of a nearby chair. 'What would you like?'

Jake lifted his shoulders in a shrug that had all the hallmarks of a casual response, yet didn't manage to entirely convince. 'Whatever you've got—I'm easy.'

Olivia released a slow breath, shaking her head slightly at his choice of words. Was he *kidding*? She glanced away for a moment and when she looked back there was an expression on Jake's face that she couldn't completely fathom. What was it? Regret? That sort of look that indicated Jake wished things could be different? That she herself could be different?

He was slipping away from her. She could sense it.

Not that she had ever really had him, of course. Such a fool to underestimate his depth of will-power, to overestimate the power of her own love for him. She had imagined her strength of feeling would be enough for them both. She had felt bold and daring, able to venture where no woman had dared venture before. But the steely exterior was too hard, too impenetrable.

She descended the stairs at a pace, trying not to dwell on what might happen in the future. At least he's here with me now, she told herself. We can spend a few hours together. And I won't ask a single question. I won't probe or pry or do anything to put what we have in jeopardy. . .

Olivia opened the refrigerator and retrieved bacon

and eggs and fresh juice. Whilst the bacon sizzled on the stove she laid two trays and then wandered into the living-room to tidy up.

Their clothes were where they'd left them; discarded in a tangled heap on the floor before the dead ashes of the fire. Slowly Olivia picked up each garment, folding them methodically, remembering with a shiver of awareness each touch, each passionate moment. His jacket had fallen behind a chair. Olivia walked over and picked it up, shaking it slightly, smoothing the creases, holding the garment to her as if Jake were still inside.

Her foot scuffed against something on the floor and Olivia caught a glimpse of a wallet before it spun away out of sight beneath a large square footstool. She bent down and retrieved the supple brown leather object, holding it in her hand for a moment, tracing Jake's gold-embossed initials with a careful finger, her eyes drawn, as if she was mesmerised, by the shiny print that protruded from beneath the clasp.

A photograph. His family? Himself?

Olivia's finger traced the worn edge, hovered uncertainly over the clasp. Would it be so terrible if she took a peek? Just a quick look. She glanced towards the stairs. Jake need never know, and, after all, it could have fallen open anyway. . .

The bacon was screaming for attention, spitting and sizzling angrily in the pan. She had turned the heat up too high as usual and it would be burned. Still holding the wallet, Olivia dashed into the kitchen and lifted the frying-pan away from the glowing hob.

Should she look? She gripped the wallet between her fingers. The temptation was overwhelming. The photograph would be important to Jake, otherwise why would he bother to carry it around with him? His family. She would see his parents. . .

With a swift, guilty movement Olivia flicked open the wallet. Just a quick look, a second to glance at their features, to spot the resemblance, nothing more. . .

There wasn't one, but two photographs to hold her attention; Jake with his parents, as she had suspected, caught in holiday mode; blue skies, golden sands, somewhere overseas. Olivia looked at it for a moment and then pulled out the second.

Deep down she had half dreaded finding a picture of Sophie, so why did she feel so surprised, so hurt now? The camera had caught the two of them very well. Two laughing, smiling individuals, a younger, sweeter-looking Sophie without a care in the world laughing up into Jake's bronzed handsome face. His arms were around her slim body in an unmistakably intimate embrace. He looked like another person, Olivia thought; relaxed, happy, devoted.

Olivia stared at the image for a long while, forgetting the bacon, forgetting everything else. She didn't think it was possible to feel so much emotional pain.

Then she remembered the other photo, the one she had purloined from the dresser in Jake's kitchen almost two weeks ago now. She had slipped it into her purse when she had returned home that same day. Olivia moved to the hook on the back of the kitchen door and rummaged swiftly, pulling out the small square passport photo in order to compare and examine.

All three photographs had been taken at around the same time. She closed her eyes tight for a moment, dropping the wallet onto the kitchen table in despair. *Hell*!

She had convinced herself of Jake's innocent involvement; he had helped convince her—he had told her that he and Sophie had never been lovers. Now what could she think except that he had been...*was* behaving in the most despicable way imaginable? She had forced herself to believe Sophie's feelings for Jake to be a simple—or even not so simple—infatuation. An intense crush that had been complicated by the death of his family.

But not this. Olivia's eyes lingered over the photograph again, over the clear mutual adoration. Not such love...

Had he simply tired of her? Had his parents' death been a catalyst for change?

Whatever, he was clearly playing games with both of them—she was being as big a fool as Sophie.

With a stifled sob Olivia picked up the photographs and pushed them back into the wallet. What should she do? She wanted very much to storm upstairs and confront him; to yell and shout. But to make a scene? Like Sophie? Olivia shook her head determinedly, remembering the pity she had witnessed on Jake's face at the May ball. No. Never that. She would be dignified. Now was her chance to claw back some of her tattered pride.

Swiftly she went into the living-room and pushed the wallet into the jacket. Jake must never know she had seen the evidence of his deceit. Never.

'What happened to the bacon?'

Olivia set the tray down onto the bedside table with extra care. 'I... I burned it, I'm afraid,' she murmured unsteadily. 'I never was much of a cook.' She began pouring the coffee. She glanced nervously across. Could he see her hands shaking?

'Well, toast will do.' He picked a slice from the plate,

frowning a little at the charred edges. 'I see you like it well done.' His gaze rested speculatively on Olivia's taut face for a moment, then he glanced towards the window. 'I thought maybe we could go for a walk this morning. It looks as if it's going to be a beautiful day. I'll show you the estate. . .afterwards you can take a proper look at the downstairs rooms—'

'I. . . I don't think so.' Olivia picked up a fragrant mug of coffee, cursing beneath her breath as some of its contents spilled onto the tray.

Jake watched for a moment as Olivia dabbed distractedly with a paper towel. 'OK, we'll drive, then.'

'No!' Olivia inhaled an urgent breath. 'I mean. . . I've changed my mind about the village tour. I was thinking downstairs about. . .about everything,' she continued stiltedly, 'and you were right, I have tended to jump in rather too quickly. Being a busybody around the village, interfering with the way you want to run your life—'

'I can't believe I'm hearing this!' Jake took a mouthful of coffee. 'Are you serious?' Dark eyes followed Olivia as she walked around and sat on the far edge of the bed. 'You certainly look it,' he drawled. His mouth twisted slightly. 'Hey, I thought the idea was to have breakfast *in* bed! Olivia?' He frowned, releasing a long-drawn-out breath when she made no move. 'Look, I know I was angry last night. But last night I was tired and I lost my temper. This morning I'm OK about the idea.' He waited a moment for a response and when Olivia still didn't reply he added sharply, 'If you're worried that I'll change my mind at a later stage, then don't be. Being fickle isn't one of my bad points—'

'Isn't it?'

He looked at her carefully, his eyes narrowing in

scrutiny. 'You seem edgy all of a sudden,' he murmured conversationally. 'What's the matter?'

Olivia looked away. It was murderous meeting Jake's searching gaze. 'I. . . I told you, downstairs I've been thinking about everything—'

'Everything?' There was a slight pause. 'Something tells me that that includes our relationship.'

Olivia steeled herself and, finding the courage from somewhere, turned back towards him. She gripped the mug firmly in her hands and felt the heat of the coffee burning her palms. 'Our. . .arrangement, yes.'

'Our arrangement.' He repeated her words with cool precision. 'And what have you concluded—care to tell me?' His enquiry was utterly controlled. The dark ebony eyes were suddenly as hard as ice. 'You have concluded something,' he continued. 'I think I can guess what it is by the look on your face and the choice of your words, but I'd like you to tell me anyway.'

'I'm. . .' Olivia released a breath and then took a gulp of scalding coffee. 'I'm not. . .interested in continuing our. . .our relationship any more, Jake.' She glanced across at him and tilted her chin a little, remembering her tattered pride. 'I thought I was, but I'm not.'

His mouth twisted chillingly. 'And that's it?'

Olivia frowned, as if enduring physical pain. 'Isn't that enough?' She rose from the bed and spun away towards the window. 'You've taken everything from me! What more do you want?'

'It's a swift decision,' he drawled. 'Ten minutes ago you left the room smiling. How about an explanation?' His voice was ominously mild.

'I've been seeing someone else.' She hadn't planned to say it. To lie so audaciously. She loved him with all her heart, she *had* loved him, and yet she wanted to hurt him so badly. Would he believe the lie? Olivia wondered. Would he even care?

'I see.'

Not a drop of emotion in his voice. Olivia turned towards Jake, her eyes lingering helplessly over the magnificent bronze torso with its expanse of curly dark hair.

'Did you hear what I said?' Olivia's voice wobbled alarmingly. She cleared her throat and tried to appear as if she were in control. 'Jake?'

'I heard.'

Sick despair overwhelmed her suddenly. 'So it's over, then.' She began moving towards the bedroom door. 'I. . . I think you'd better go.'

Jake's dark eyes pinned her to the spot. 'Who is he?'

Olivia halted, her blue eyes widened in alarm. 'What?'

The hard mouth curved. 'You heard me; I'm enquiring about your other lover.'

'You don't want to know.' Olivia gulped a breath and then opened the door. 'I'd like you to leave,' she murmured shakily. 'Now. . .please!'

'When you've given me a name,' Jake drawled. 'When you've convinced me.'

'I don't need to convince you of anything!' Olivia retorted angrily. 'I've told you I'm seeing someone else—that should be enough!'

'It isn't.' He surveyed her with aggravating mildness. 'I don't believe you.'

She hadn't expected this—all sorts of possibilities, but not this. Had her foolish devotion been so obvious, then?

'You ignored me for nine days whilst you were

gallivanting around Europe with Sophie!' Olivia
retorted angrily. 'What do you think I did? Stayed in
every night, waiting by the phone like a besotted
schoolgirl?' She gulped a shaky breath. That was vir-
tually what she had done. Olivia lowered her head to
hide the tears. 'I wanted you and you weren't there. . .'
She couldn't get the photograph out of her mind. 'I. . .
I told you before, I'm. . . I'm no angel.'

'The man you worked with in London—was it him?'
Jake's voice was as hard as steel now. Clearly the
unthinkable was becoming a possibility. 'Did he call by
on the off-chance whilst I was away, is that it?'

Olivia felt the beginnings of fear; she had taken an
unnecessary, dangerous path. What was the point in
this ridiculous lie? Jake Savage could muster supreme
control when it suited—but what about when it didn't
suit—what then?

'Olivia! Look at me, damn you!' He flung back the
bedclothes and crossed the room towards her, looming
above her slim figure, strong and tanned and full of
power, gripping her by the shoulders, shaking her. 'Is
that what happened?'

He still couldn't quite bring himself to believe it—
maybe he did care about her a little, then. Or was it
the thought that another man had laid claim to her
body, whilst he had imagined himself to have full and
sole possession of it, that gave his face such a fearful
look of savage anger?

All it would take to finish their relationship, Olivia
saw, would be an infinitesimal nod of her head.

She did it quickly. Better to end the pain of loving
Jake now. He wouldn't want her after this admission.
The very real danger that she might change her mind

and put up with the humiliation and deceit and continue their relationship was finally at an end.

Jake's ego would never allow him to endure such a fate.

He stared down at her for a long moment, his features strained and rigid with the effort of keeping control. Then he spun away and left the room, while Olivia hung her head and began to cry.

'You're coming with me!'

She wasn't sure how many minutes she had been lying face down on the bed sobbing; long enough to imagine that Jake had left the cottage, to relive the foolishness of her actions, to scan the future, to hate what she saw. . .

His grip was fierce and without mercy. He hauled Olivia bodily to her feet, not releasing her, shaking her a little, so that in her surprise she sagged against him like a worn-out rag doll. 'Stand up!' He shook her again and gradually Olivia came to her senses. She rubbed her glistening cheeks with the back of her hand and stared up into Jake's angry face.

'What. . .what are you doing?'

'Get dressed!' He pulled her around the room to the wardrobe and flung open one of the doors. 'Put something on. You're coming with me.'

'Where?' Olivia frowned in amazement. 'What are you talking about?'

'Just do as I say, Olivia,' he gritted, 'or, God help me, I won't be responsible for my actions!'

'You can't treat me like this!' Olivia gulped a breath and tried to stifle a sob with her hand. 'I don't want to go anywhere with you. I told you it's over!'

'Oh, no!' He shook his head and tugged her sharply

towards his body, holding her head with his other hand, forcing her to survey the rage in his face. 'Not yet, it isn't! Our relationship's over when I say so, and not before.'

'You're. . .hurting me!' Olivia tried to twist free of his grasp. 'Please. . . Jake!'

'Do you love me?' Olivia stilled at his words, her heart thudding to a halt in her chest. Jake tugged her closer, so that she could feel the masculine strength of him against every contour of her body. '*Do* you?' He looked fierce. Wild. She had never seen him like this before.

She nodded. Suddenly denial seemed pointless.

'Say it!'

Tears filled Olivia's eyes and spilled over onto her cheeks. 'I. . .love you.'

He didn't seem satisfied. Had he *wanted* to hear the truth?

'Get dressed.' He released her and moved towards the window. Olivia stood a moment, staring at the broad back. She felt as if her legs were going to buckle beneath her at any minute. She gripped the edge of the wardrobe door for support and picked one of the hangers at random.

The two minutes or so it took for Olivia to slip on the flame-coloured dress seemed to make a difference to Jake's temper. When he turned it was clear that some of the control had returned.

'Where are we going?' He had taken her hand and was leading her resolutely down the stairs.

'To my home.'

He drove in silence. Olivia didn't dare speak. He might have regained control, but he was still furious. She glanced behind at his jacket, thrown angrily onto the rear seat as he had got in, and forced herself to picture the photograph of Jake and Sophie.

His house felt cold and unlived-in. Olivia reminded herself that he had been away and that Sophie had gone with him too.

'In here.' The grand downstairs rooms looked just as bleak as the last time she had laid eyes on them. Jake moved towards one of the windows and flung back the curtains.

'What are we doing here?' Olivia's voice sounded small and insignificant in the high-ceilinged room. 'I told you, I'm abandoning the village tour—'

'You think I'm interested in *that*?' He looked scornful. 'Find my wallet!' He threw his jacket towards Olivia, who reached out a hand and caught it automatically. 'You should know where it is—you replaced it in one of the pockets after you looked at it. Go on!' He glared at her. 'I think you'll find it's in the outside right.'

Olivia's fingers gripped the cloth. She stared across at Jake's rigid face in dismay. 'I don't. . .want to find it.'

'But why on earth not?' He walked towards her. 'I thought you liked looking at family snapshots. There are a couple in there that you're sure to find interesting.' He removed his jacket from her grasp and produced the wallet. 'What's wrong, Olivia?' he murmured softly. 'Don't you want to take a look?'

She took a steadying breath. 'I've seen them.'

'I know.' He regarded Olivia steadily for a moment. 'Care to tell me what conclusions you jumped to?'

'I didn't jump to any conclusions!' Olivia responded sharply. 'The photograph of you and Sophie spoke for itself.'

'Did it, indeed?'

'Jake, I don't see the point in all this,' Olivia continued miserably. 'I know it was wrong of me to look inside your wallet, but. . .but you lied to me.' She raised watery blue eyes to his face and then looked away, hating his cold, hard gaze. 'I believed you,' she murmured, 'when you said that you hated deceit. I tried to understand when you told me that you didn't want a complicated relationship. I *trusted* you when you said there would be no one else. . .'

'There hasn't been anyone else!'

'What do you take me for—a fool?' Olivia flared. 'You lied about Sophie!'

'I did not lie.' Jake moved past Olivia and pulled the dust sheet off an ornate secretaire that was positioned in the far corner of the room. He wrenched open a drawer and, after some moments of searching, finally pulled out a large square book.

'The family album,' he announced. 'You like looking at photographs, Olivia; come and take a look at these.'

'Why are you being like this?' Olivia asked, shaking her head. 'What little we had together is over. It's finished.'

Jet eyes pierced her face. 'You told me you loved me—wasn't that the truth?'

Olivia threw him an anguished look. 'What do you want—blood?' she cried. 'I've given you everything, Jake, *everything*! Don't ask for any more!' She shook her head wildly. 'I can't continue torturing myself over a man who's only interested in me for one reason and one reason only!'

'You really think that's how it's been?'

'You made it perfectly plain—'

'Yes, I did, didn't I?' The sensual mouth curved into an odd, self-deprecating smile. 'So. . .what happens if I admit to you that I've been a fool—what then?' Jake continued quietly. Olivia stared blankly, confused, more than anything, by the sudden quiet intensity in Jake's voice. Her throat ached with unshed tears. 'Shall I tell you a little about my life, Olivia?' he asked. He quirked a dark brow when Olivia made no reply and she saw the hint of derision at his lips. 'Nothing to say? Ah, well, I'll tell you anyway, I know it's what you want, even if you do seem rather unwilling to admit it now.' He inhaled a ragged sort of breath. 'First the infamous love affair.' His lips curved mirthlessly as he rested his gaze on Olivia's taut features. 'A short, but extremely intense involvement with a woman who didn't want me, only my lifestyle.' He gave a harsh laugh. 'I fell in love with a gold-digger—or at least at the time it *felt* like love. . .' He stared at her. 'Practically the whole of the county knew what she was, but not me. In two short months I bestowed enough jewels and expensive trinkets upon her for her to start her own shop! Luckily I saw the light just before I made a complete fool of myself and proposed marriage—'

'What. . .happened?' Olivia asked carefully.

'Nothing dramatic.' Jake's look was ironic. 'Considering how I felt inside, the end of our relationship was rather feeble. I was in London on business,' he explained, 'and I saw her coming out of an hotel with a man.'

'It wasn't. . .' Olivia lifted her shoulders slightly '. . .her brother?'

Jake's mouth twisted wryly. 'No, it wasn't. And then,' he continued stiltedly, 'three weeks later, whilst I was still coming to terms with having made a complete idiot of myself, my family were wiped off the face of the earth in one fell swoop.' There was a heart-rending silence. 'I needed her most then.' He shook his head. 'I needed *some*one.'

Olivia swallowed back her tears. 'I. . .still don't understand where guilt comes into all this,' she croaked. 'You said to me once—'

'Yes, I know what I said!' Jake thrust large hands into his trouser pockets and spun away. 'You saw the photograph of my family this morning; you know they were a handsome couple. I loved them very much,' he continued half to himself, so softly that Olivia had to step forward to catch what he said. 'Even my father— despite what he did to my mother.'

Olivia frowned. She wasn't sure she wanted to hear all this. She could see the pain, hear the rough agony in Jake's voice as he spoke. He was right, she had wanted to know everything from the first moment of meeting, but that was before she knew of the tragedies he had had to endure. 'What. . .did he do?' she asked finally, in a tremulous voice.

'He kept mistresses.' Strain clenched the dark features. 'Set them up in houses. . . There was even one in the village. He'd had her for years. . .' the hard mouth curled derisively '. . .in every sense. I found out, kept it to myself for several weeks and then one day I took it upon myself to tell my mother.'

'That can't have been. . .very pleasant.'

'That has to be the understatement of the year!' Jake's mouth twisted bitterly. 'It was a revelation. All those years they had pretended and lied about their marriage. My mother knew all along, you see. She *knew* and yet she continued to put up with it! I was very angry with my father; with my mother too. I lost my temper, said things. . .' The dark head shook again and Olivia could see he was hating himself for the things he had said. 'I felt as if we'd all been living a lie. I felt so angry with them both. The next day...' His voice hardened. 'The next day they died in the air crash.' He lifted his head and Olivia saw the tremor in the angular jaw. 'I refused to go on the trip to America with them, you see... I couldn't bear the thought of spending time with my father.' Jake threw Olivia a humourless smile. 'Lucky escape, eh?' There was a tense pause. 'My brother took my place instead.'

Olivia gulped back her tears. 'Edward.'

'Yes. Poor, kind Edward. I told you we were like chalk and cheese, didn't I?' Jake murmured. 'He wasn't a one for confrontations. He tried to keep the peace; he didn't want to upset my parents the way I had done.' Jake glanced down at the album he held. 'This hasn't seen the light of day for a long while—not since the accident. That's when I shut up these rooms; they were used by the family and I tried to forget they had ever existed.' He shook his head. 'It didn't work, of course. I spent some time travelling, but the ancestral ties always pulled me back...' He looked directly at Olivia. 'And besides, there was Sophie to feel responsible for.'

Sophie. Back to her again.

'Don't say any more, please,' Olivia whispered. 'It's difficult for you and...and I'm not sure I've got the strength to hear it—'

'For a long while I did wonder if I shouldn't marry Sophie,' Jake continued, almost oblivious of Olivia's interruption. 'We hadn't ever been particularly close, but guilt is a strong emotion—'

'Please...stop—!' Olivia tried to speak but a sob caught in her throat.

'Then I met you.' Jake closed the book with a bang and hurled it angrily across the room. 'I can't believe

I've been such a fool!' he thundered. Olivia, startled by the sudden explosive outburst, jumped dramatically. 'Go on, take a look!' he commanded roughly as he headed for the door. 'The pictures speak for themselves.'

Olivia stood trance-like for several long seconds, staring at the door Jake had banged shut behind him. Then slowly, as if in a dream, half dreading what she might discover, she picked up the photograph album and looked inside.

'Jake! Jake!' Olivia's long, slim legs flew wildly along the corridor. She had no idea which direction he had taken, but instinct told her to search for him outside.

The sun was bright and warm. Her heels clicked impatiently along the terrace. She ran towards the balustrade and scanned the extensive grounds, searching frantically for Jake's unmistakable figure.

Then she saw him across the large expanse of immaculate lawn. He was walking slowly, head bent. She called his name again and he turned to look at her, waiting whilst Olivia frantically negotiated the distance between them.

'Why. . .?' She could barely speak. Olivia stood panting breathlessly, her sapphire eyes latched on to Jake's rugged face. She licked her lips, swallowed and tried again. 'Why. . .didn't you tell me your brother was your twin?' She shook her head almost desperately. 'I. . . I saw the photograph of the two of you side by side, and I could scarcely believe it. You were practically identical.'

Jake met her gaze steadily. 'I was the elder by ten minutes.'

'And the photograph in your wallet. . .the one with Sophie?' Olivia whispered.

'That was Edward.'

It was like a weight being lifted from her shoulders. 'Sophie loved him very much, didn't she?'

'They loved each other,' Jake replied simply. 'Since childhood. That's why it's been so hard to bear for her.'

Olivia frowned as realisation dawned. 'And I suppose every time she saw you it was like seeing. . .'

'Just like seeing Edward, yes. She gets confused at times,' Jake continued. 'She started drinking not long after the accident and then. . .' He inhaled a tense breath. 'Well, it can be pretty. . .' He shrugged, lost for words suddenly.

Olivia frowned, remembering the May ball. 'Awful. Yes, I know.' She paused, feeling such joy that her worst fears had been unfounded, but miserable and helpless that Jake had, and was still suffering so. She took a step towards him and reached out, taking his hands in hers. 'I think Sophie needs help, Jake; proper treatment,' she added quietly. 'A change of environment. A complete rest, that sort of thing.'

'That's exactly what she's having.' Jake's brilliant eyes shimmered as he looked down at her. 'When I left your cottage to go with her last night we ended up having a long talk—it was the first really honest conversation we'd had since Edward's death. It was painful for both of us, but ultimately it brought us to our senses. Sophie finally understood that things couldn't go on as they had been doing.' Jake released a taut breath. 'I know it's not always appeared so, but underneath Sophie is a very sane, sensible girl; she agreed that time—a long time—spent with some relations she has in Scotland, under proper medical supervision, would be wise.'

'Do you think she'll ever want to return?' Olivia asked.

Jake considered carefully. 'I doubt it. Maybe.' He gazed at Olivia steadily and she felt the instant, overwhelming intensity of his gaze. 'You understand now that she's never loved me. It's only ever been Edward.'

'Yes.' Olivia's voice wobbled alarmingly. 'Oh, Jake! All this *time*! All this time and I thought—!'

Jake raised her hands to his lips and kissed her fingers very gently. 'We've barely known each other two weeks.'

'It feels like a lifetime,' Olivia replied unsteadily, feeling desire flare as he pulled her towards him. 'I mean. . .' she corrected swiftly.

The stunning mouth curved into a smile that warmed her heart. 'I know what you mean,' he murmured. He touched her face, gazing down at her with such tenderness that Olivia wanted to weep. 'Do you know I loved you the first moment I saw you?'

His admission shocked Olivia into stillness. She stared, wide-eyed, surveying the handsome, compelling face in amazement. 'You did?' She felt the rush of salty tears filling her eyes. 'In the lane, even before we—?'

'Even before we made love,' Jake finished. 'Yes. Even then. Don't cry, sweetheart.' He lifted a hand and brushed her cheek gently. 'You've made me very happy.'

'I have?'

'You find it hard to believe?' The firm mouth twisted in warm amusement. 'I didn't want to believe it myself at first. Seeing you. . .wanting you so desperately. . . I was frightened of making a fool of myself again. . .'

Jake's voice trailed away a little as he remembered. 'But you managed to bring me such instantaneous joy. After all the misery, all the guilt. . . I didn't think I deserved it. I wasn't sure I could trust it. . . But I was weak, you made me weak,' he added with a smile, 'and I couldn't resist, so I came up with this stupid idea that it was simply sexual. Except that it wasn't simple at all, because there was so much more. . .' He paused and then added softly, 'When I first saw you I felt as if it was—'

'Meant to be?' Olivia beamed up at the strong, handsome face, rejoicing at his words.

'How did you know?' Jake's mouth widened into a huge smile and for the first time Olivia saw that he was truly happy.

'Easy,' she murmured, standing on tiptoe to kiss his mouth. 'I experienced that special feeling too.'

'You did?' Jake pulled her close, circling her body with his arms, kissing her mouth with a slow, lingering sexuality. 'That's interesting. And what. . .' he kissed her again, deeper this time, with more intensity '. . .is this special feeling called?'

Olivia gazed up into the stunning face and felt the surge of overwhelming love. 'Destiny,' she told him solemnly.

'Always meant to be?' Jake queried huskily, holding her close.

'Absolutely,' Olivia murmured, kissing the expressive mouth. 'Always and forever.'

'Will you marry me?' Jake held her face in his hands and kissed her mouth tenderly. 'Will you live here and make me the happiest man alive?'

'Of course.' Olivia's eyes sparkled with happiness. 'I thought you'd never ask.'

# EPILOGUE

OLIVIA strolled into the library, chose a favourite book and wandered outside into the garden. She probably wouldn't manage to read more than a few pages without Faith yelling for attention, but that didn't matter—the idea of relaxing quietly for a few moments with a book on her lap on such a wonderful summer evening as this was a treat in itself.

The chairs were already positioned expectantly on the balcony, piled high with cushions. Olivia eased herself gently into one of them and surveyed the magnificent expanse of well-tended garden and parkland, which looked so beautiful bathed in the last few rays of late August sun.

A sound of footsteps made her turn. She smiled as Jake emerged from the house, aware of the surge of love that hadn't diminished with time, and tilted her head expectantly as he bent and kissed her tenderly on the lips.

'You're looking very pleased with yourself,' Olivia murmured softly, glowing as his mouth lingered on her skin, as his hand briefly touched the slight swelling of her stomach.

'And why not?' he drawled softly, contemplating Olivia's happy face. 'I have just succeeded in putting to sleep in record time the sweetest baby daughter a man could have.'

'Clever old you!' Olivia's mouth widened in delighted surprise. 'How did you manage that?'

'Oh, my talents have no bounds.' Jake kissed her lightly again, before sitting in the chair beside her. 'Actually, I think I bored her to sleep.'

Olivia chuckled. 'How?'

'I read one of my veterinary manuals in the most soothing voice I could muster. It did the trick. Faith was asleep after the fourth page.' His mouth curved attractively. 'She's a smart girl; even at this young age she figured sleep was a better alternative than listening to the care and methods of treating horses with laminitis.'

Olivia frowned. 'Lami-*what*?'

Jake smiled. 'It doesn't matter. She's asleep now, that's the main thing.' Dark, seductive eyes travelled over Olivia's figure and rested eventually on her face. 'How are you feeling now? Better?'

She nodded. 'Much better. I haven't felt sick for at least an hour.' Olivia positioned herself more comfortably in her chair and reached out a hand towards her husband. 'Do you know how happy I am?' she asked softly.

Ebony eyes gleamed knowingly. 'I could hazard a pretty good guess.' He linked his fingers with hers. 'Sweetheart, I'm so pleased you're pregnant again,' he murmured huskily. He reached forward and placed the flat of his hand on Olivia's stomach. 'I know it's pretty soon after having Faith but—'

'No buts.' Olivia pressed a finger to Jake's lips. 'Carrying your child. . .you must know how wonderful that makes me feel.'

'You're beautiful.' Jake rose from his chair and pulled Olivia gently to her feet. 'The only woman in the world for me.' He lowered his head and kissed her upturned face with a slow, lingering sexuality. 'I want us to have a hundred children.'

'I may not be able to manage that.' Olivia entwined her fingers around Jake's neck as the surge of sensual desire moved through her. 'But I won't object to trying. Let's go to bed, darling,' she whispered.

'Will it be all right?' Jake's mouth covered hers again and she tasted the glorious moist warmth of him. 'You saw the doctor today; did she say—?'

'She said it would be fine.' Olivia stroked Jake's face with a fingertip, revelling in the hard, solid strength of his body. 'Just fine.'

The sensuous mouth curved. 'Thank heaven for that!' Jake lifted her in one easy movement into his arms, cradling her gently against his solid, masculine frame. 'Patience was never one of my finer points,' he drawled. 'These last six weeks have felt like an eternity.'

'You think I haven't noticed?' Olivia teased.

He moved with slow purpose towards the house, carrying a blissful Olivia up the wide curving staircase to the door of their room, pausing only briefly once they were inside, kissing Olivia softly on the mouth, relishing the taste of her. 'Forever, darling,' he murmured.

And, as he laid her on the bed and began to remove her clothes with reverent hands, Olivia knew that he meant it.

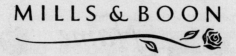

# MILLS & BOON

## Next Month's Romances

Each month you can choose from a wide variety of romance with Mills & Boon. Below are the new titles to look out for next month.

| | |
|---|---|
| LAST STOP MARRIAGE | Emma Darcy |
| RELATIVE SINS | Anne Mather |
| HUSBAND MATERIAL | Emma Goldrick |
| A FAULKNER POSSESSION | Margaret Way |
| UNTAMED LOVER | Sharon Kendrick |
| A SIMPLE TEXAS WEDDING | Ruth Jean Dale |
| THE COLORADO COUNTESS | Stephanie Howard |
| A NIGHT TO REMEMBER | Anne Weale |
| TO TAME A PROUD HEART | Cathy Williams |
| SEDUCED BY THE ENEMY | Kathryn Ross |
| PERFECT CHANCE | Amanda Carpenter |
| CONFLICT OF HEARTS | Liz Fielding |
| A PAST TO DENY | Kate Proctor |
| NO OBJECTIONS | Kate Denton |
| HEADING FOR TROUBLE! | Linda Miles |
| WHITE MIDNIGHT | Kathleen O'Brien |

*Available from WH Smith, John Menzies, Volume One, Forbuoys, Martins, Woolworths, Tesco, Asda, Safeway and other paperback stockists.*

# Name that Song

How would you like to win a year's supply of simply irresistible romances? Well, you can and they're free! Simply solve the puzzle below and send your completed entry to us by 31st October 1996. The first five correct entries picked after the closing date will each win a years supply of Temptation novels (four books every month—worth over £100).

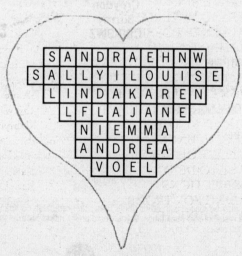

| S | A | N | D | R | A | E | H | N | W |
|---|---|---|---|---|---|---|---|---|---|
| S | A | L | L | Y | I | L | O | U | I | S | E |
| L | I | N | D | A | K | A | R | E | N |
| L | F | L | A | J | A | N | E |
| N | I | E | M | M | A |
| A | N | D | R | E | A |
| V | O | E | L |

*Please turn over for details of how to enter* ☞

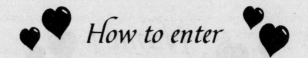

# How to enter

To solve our puzzle...first circle eight well known girls names hidden in the grid. Then unscramble the remaining letters to reveal the title of a well-known song (five words).

When you have written the song title in the space provided below, don't forget to fill in your name and address, pop this page into an envelope (you don't need a stamp) and post it today! Hurry—competition ends 31st October 1996.

**Mills & Boon Song Puzzle
FREEPOST
Croydon
Surrey
CR9 3WZ**

Song Title: _____

Are you a Reader Service Subscriber?   Yes ❏    No ❏

Ms/Mrs/Miss/Mr _____

Address _____

_____

_____ Postcode _____

One application per household.

You may be mailed with other offers from other reputable companies as a result of this application. If you would prefer not to receive such offers, please tick box.   ❏

C396
D